G000080337

This is the first novel from David Black who writes under his late mother's maiden name. David hails from the Isle of Wight and has a simple philosophy to life:
doubt everything, find your own light.

He says; 'The idea for this book has been circulating around my head for the past ten years; I started writing it eight years ago.

'The story of Lady Jane Grey has fascinated many since her death and exemplifies the complexity brutality of the Tudor reign and others before and after it; with religious persuasion and a lust for power being the overriding reason for the rise, fall and often death of many.

'There are many aspects of the accounts of Jane's life which do not make sense but the one that set me off on this path was the fact that nowhere is there a verified painting, from the time, of Lady Jane Grey; that seemed odd to me for a former queen of England; albeit for only nine days.'

I would like to thank Lucy Ellis, who has contributed massively to the content of this book, particularly at a time when I was struggling a little with its direction.

Lucy Ellis is an author of sixteen years, published in a variety of genres; she has seven full-length biographies, a music critique, thirteen eBooks, four self-help memoirs and countless blogs.

This venture was Lucy's first foray into fiction.

I dedicated this book to my late mother Eyvonne.
Her love of books and reading was cruelly curtailed by Parkinson's disease.
Mum; for life, and love, thank you X

David Black

Before the Reign Falls

The Lost Words of Lady Jane Grey

Copyright © David Black (2017)

The right of David Black to be identified as author of this work has been asserted by him in accordance with section 77 and 78 of the Copyright, Designs and Patents Act 1988.

All rights reserved. No part of this publication may be reproduced, stored in a retrieval system, or transmitted in any form or by any means, electronic, mechanical, photocopying, recording, or otherwise, without the prior permission of the publishers.

Any person who commits any unauthorized act in relation to this publication may be liable to criminal prosecution and civil claims for damages.

A CIP catalogue record for this title is available from the British Library.

ISBN 9781785548536 (Paperback)
ISBN 9781785548543 (Hardback)
ISBN 9781785548550 (eBook)

www.austinmacauley.com

First Published (2017)
Austin Macauley Publishers Ltd.
25 Canada Square
Canary Wharf
London
E14 5LQ

Prologue

Lady Jane Grey, the Nine Days' Queen, was executed at the age of sixteen on a chilly February morning in 1554, by order of Queen Mary I. Jane's tragedy was a heady mix of her diluted royal blood, years of political posturing, callous scheming parents and her own precocious and, some would say, belligerent nature.

In 1509, the popular eighteen-year-old prince known for his love of hunting and the arts, took to the throne as King Henry VIII. Inheriting a stable realm with healthy finances, during his youth Henry VIII distanced himself from ruling matters, relying heavily on trusted counsel from Thomas Wolsey who became both Lord Chancellor and Cardinal in 1515. Henry VIII married Catherine of Aragon just months after his ascension and, while the union produced six children (including three boys), only one heir survived: a girl named Mary. Some twenty years later Henry's long-suffering wife was deemed past her childbearing years and, coincidentally, the king had fallen for Catherine's lady-in-waiting, Anne Boleyn: an annulment to his marriage was sought from the pope.

When Wolsey failed to secure the king's marital freedom, it expedited the end of his career as well as his life and Henry turned to Wolsey's apprentice, Thomas Cromwell, as his new adviser. Distraught at the death of his mentor and desperate to secure his own future, Cromwell masterminded the reformation which initiated the break from Rome and established King Henry VIII as the head of the Church of England, as well as enabling the divorce. Over the next few years, monasteries and churches were destroyed in the dissolution, with the treasures being confiscated by the crown and the land sold to the gentry.

While Henry remained Catholic, the public were increasingly turning to Protestantism.

Henry's second marriage was performed with some haste as Anne Boleyn was pregnant with an heir: a girl named Elizabeth. A few subsequent miscarriages later, including one believed to be a son, Henry became convinced that the union was cursed and so his wife was spuriously accused of the treasonable offence of adultery and publicly beheaded.

Meanwhile, Henry had taken Anne's lady-in-waiting, Jane Seymour, as his third wife. This pairing finally produced a male heir, Edward in 1537, but Jane died soon after childbirth. Cromwell then mismatched his king with the German princess, Anne of Cleves, but found himself executed for treason when the marriage was swiftly annulled having not been consummated. Henry's fifth wife, Anne's teenage lady-in-waiting Katherine Howard, was executed on grounds of adultery, while his final wife, Catherine Parr, failed to produce a royal heir, but survived the king's death.

As Henry's only son, Edward ascended to the throne as Edward VI, upon his father's demise in 1547, ahead of his two older half-sisters who were deemed to be illegitimate given their mothers' falls from grace. Aged just nine, Edward initially ruled through the council of regency Henry VIII had created however, without a strong king in command, the noblemen jostled for superiority and Edward Seymour, the boy's eldest uncle, proclaimed himself Lord Protector. During the following years, Roman Catholic practices were eradicated and the Church of England became increasingly Protestant under the young king's direction. There followed a rebellion in Norfolk, which Seymour was unable to handle, leaving him exposed. John Dudley, the Earl of Warwick, seized the opportunity to overthrow the Lord Protector, and Seymour was arrested and later executed.

Dudley amplified the Protestant reform and manipulated a new heir to the throne when the fifteen-year-old king became seriously ill with tuberculosis.

In June 1553, Dudley persuaded the dying king to subvert the claims of his older half-sisters, Mary and Elizabeth, under the Third Succession Act by nominating the successor to the crown as his first-cousin-once-removed: the great-granddaughter of Henry VII, and Dudley's recently-acquired daughter-in-law, the Protestant Lady Jane Grey.

Edward VI died on 6 July 1553 and four days later, Lady Jane Grey was proclaimed queen. However, the king's last acts were controversial and, backed by public support, the Privy Council decided to change sides and proclaimed Henry VIII's eldest daughter, the Catholic Mary, as queen on 19 July 1553. Dudley quickly lost support and even the deposed-queen's own father acknowledged the new monarch in a bid to save his life.

Lady Jane Grey and her husband were imprisoned in the Tower of London and tried for high treason in November 1553; Jane pleaded guilty – although innocently so, not by intent – and was handed a suspended death sentence. Her fate was finally sealed in February 1554, when her father unwittingly implicated her through his support of Sir Thomas Wyatt's religious rebellion opposing Mary's proposed marriage to Philip of Spain.

However, of all the kings, queens, noblemen, scholars and vagabonds whose faces illustrate our history books, art galleries and stately homes, no validated portrait of Lady Jane Grey exists to this day. In 2006, the National Portrait Gallery purchased a painting that was believed to be of Lady Jane Grey, but was derided by controversial constitutional historian, Dr David Starkey, who said, "It's an appallingly bad picture and there's absolutely no reason to suppose it's got anything to do with Lady Jane Grey. There is no documentary evidence, no evidence from inventories, jewellery or heraldry to support the idea this is Lady Jane Grey."

Lady Jane Grey was a central character in one of the most elaborate stories of the debauched Tudor dynasty, so how could this situation have arisen?

The evidence that Queen Mary I was unhappy with sanctioning the execution of her young cousin is well-documented; she was pressured to do so by her husband to be the zealous Catholic Phillip II of Spain, and his cronies who persuaded Mary that plotters against her would rally around Jane and pose a continued threat to her reign. So besotted was Mary with Phillip, that she acquiesced to his proposal, but Mary realised that Jane had nothing to do with the plot against her.

Condemned

The narrow slit opening delivered a harsh shard of light, uninvited, into the cold, damp stone chamber. This slither of first light broke through the early-morning mist and signalled the arrival of a day in February which was destined to be different from any other I had known thus far.

The early-morning stillness was broken by the distant sounds of traders; voices of people going through the motions of daily life began filtering up from the streets below. Time persists, relentless, and the day was dawning like clockwork.

Momentarily anaesthetised from my situation, I dry heaved when the stark reality hit me that the day was planned to be my last. My stomach tightened and I felt my body wrack with convulsions, but there was no relief. Despite resigned acceptance of my fate, as I absorbed the growing chorus that accompanied the city's sunrise I could not quell the anger and frustration that raged inside of me at the hand I had been dealt.

I had been trying to right a wrong as much as escape the harsh life of a poor labourer, but as the cell became brighter I would have given anything to be loading loaves on to a bread cart, dealing with fish sellers in the market or simply wandering the narrow streets in search of my next meal. Somehow I felt it would have been better if my sentence had been the result of a cunningly-hatched plan or some grand deceit, but I'm ashamed to admit that my predicament was due to a chance encounter and a search for the truth, spurred on by matters of the heart.

A memory of a face, once so beautiful, now lingered in my mind like a rotting fish in a scented lady's chamber. It was an image that I couldn't help but notice, one which subsequently signalled a drastic change in my fortunes. I did not seek this turn in my life, nor chase fame and fortune through an ingenuously clever strategy: where I find myself today is the result of a series of events that blossomed from that one brief glance which I couldn't let pass me by.

What's done is done, and I have to face the brutal consequences of my innocent pursuit of the truth alone.

Part I

Chapter One

House of Shadows

A scream broke the air. The men turned to find Alice spluttering and frantically swiping her hands across her face.

The blistering June heat had not helped the mood in the cramped car which was more suited to the Italian Riviera than the dusty Norfolk countryside.

"What does the Sat Nav say?" asked Elliot for the third time.

"I told you, it says the house is just up here on the right," snapped Alice. "But it also says that this is supposed to be a road, which it clearly isn't!"

Alice's head was still ringing from being driven on the motorways well over the speed limit with the roof off, and she was now feeling every bump of the country lanes in her boyfriend's ridiculously expensive sports car. The wild goose chase they were on to find his friend's house was not currently her idea of fun.

"What was that for?" she screamed as the convertible lurched sideways.

"Stupid pheasants, they don't move fast enough," stated Elliot as he swung the vehicle back.

"If you slowed down a little, they might stand a chance," counselled Alice.

Slamming the steering wheel with his hand, Elliot muttered something and continued to charge round the hairpin bends.

"Elliot, please slow down! I know I said I'd like to get there soon, but I'd also like to get there soon and in one piece."

Biting the inside of his cheeks, Elliot focussed on the road ahead in order to control his temper. Alice, however, was unable to restrain herself and kept yelling at him about his driving, which eventually elicited a volley of throwaway barbs and empty threats on both sides. A passing point appeared in which Elliot screeched to halt, locking both their seatbelts and causing minor whiplash. The couple stared straight ahead, each unable to find non-inflammatory words to break the tension. A few minutes passed as they sat listening to the inane chitchat of a radio phone-in show, and both parties became more conciliatory.

It was Elliot who broke the ice by asking Alice to pass the sun cream from the glove compartment: the midday rays felt like they were honing in on the back of his neck. As he rubbed the lotion on his burning skin, Alice studied the map.

"I'm sorry, sweetheart," he conceded as he handed the bottle back to her. "John's my oldest friend and he's tickled pink with this new project of his. Perhaps I should have come up here on my own, but I thought you'd enjoy the countryside and history. Instead we're hopelessly lost, have feck all reception and I'm frying in this heat." He held the top of his head to protect his scalp as the rays penetrated his short fair hair.

'Feck' was a word Elliot used a lot, courtesy of his Irish friend John who also uses it frequently as Alice would discover.

"You can borrow my scarf it you want?" Alice suggested to lighten the mood. "I'm sorry. I'm hot and bothered too, but I shouldn't have taken it out on you. It's just you know I don't like it when you go too fast." Alice regretted the dig the second it left her lips and spoke fast to avoid a repeat row.

"Anyway, I've checked John's instructions against the map and I really do think it's just up here. I think we're coming up to this junction here, in which case the turning should be on the left and then we're nearly there." She proffered the map for Elliot's approval, "See?"

"I'll take your word for it." He unclenched his hand and held it out as a peace offering. "Truce?"

"Truce," she agreed, avoiding the sweaty shake and giving him a perfunctory kiss on the lips instead. To further lighten the mood, she proffered, "I like the word feck, it can be used in the same way as the similarly spelt other words but isn't as horrid. It even has a humorous element to it."

"It doesn't mean the same," said Elliot, "although it is a euphemistic substitute but is more family friendly"

Alice's orientation skills proved accurate at last and, as Elliot navigated his precious car along the last half mile of unpaved track, the 'house' John had bought loomed ahead.

"Good God, what a tip! What has the silly fecker gone and done?" he marvelled in disbelief.

The noisy engine announced their arrival and their host rushed to the front door. His sizeable bulk blocked half the entrance as he stood with his arms outstretched, welcoming the couple. "At last, where have you been?" he asked rhetorically. "I was expecting you ages ago: welcome, welcome." The enthusiasm in John's voice was palpable. He was desperate to show his oldest friend his latest acquisition; a run-down Tudor mansion in Cawston, a tiny village in the heart of Norfolk.

"I thought I'd lost you. It's not that difficult to find is it?" he asked Elliot.

"No, not if you provide clear directions and instruct visitors to hire a tractor at the Suffolk border. We took the scenic route, shall we say. You certainly are off the beaten track – we kept missing the turning for the impossibly long dirt road you call a driveway."

John looked uncomfortable as he ran his hand through his unruly black hair. "Well, you're here now, that's the main thing. Come here," he said, embracing Elliot with a bear hug and ruffle of the head. He then turned his attention to the pretty brunette trying to get out of the lowered car with some dignity.

"Alice, I take it?" He extended his hand to help her, and lent in for a kiss on the cheek. "I'm in trouble if it's not, or rather Elliot is!" he said with a wink, allowing his Irish accent to smooth over his mischievous remark. "Come on, I'll give you the grand tour. It's old, but was magnificent once - much like myself!" he joked, admiring the ruin in front of him. Alice was a little in awe of such a larger-than-life character, but warmed to his self-deprecating style. As she absorbed the ramshackle remains of the mansion in all its glory, she couldn't help but wonder if it was even worth renovating. Forcing a smile, she tried to think of something polite to say to her host. "It's, um… got a lot of potential," she offered.

"That is has! Elliot tells me you're a historian, Alice? This should be right up your street then, it being old and all that," he beamed, ignorant of her disdain.

"Well, yes and no. British medieval history is not quite the same as Egyptian hieroglyphics. The script I study was developed some three thousand years or more before Christ, and used a system of numeration up to a million, so something that has only been around for a few hundred years doesn't quite cut it with me as being very old, I'm afraid. Hieroglyphs were called, by the Egyptians, 'the words of God' and were used mainly by the priests. These painstakingly drawn symbols–"

"Point taken," conceded John. "Sorry Alice, I get it, Tudor houses are not your thing."

"It's not that they are not my thing," she said, backtracking, "it's just that…"

"OK, OK," mediated Elliot. "Alice, you are a celebrated historian reading Egyptian hieroglyphics at Oxford, and a bit too feisty for your own good sometimes; John, this wreck of a Tudor house is your new project and we're here to marvel at what an idiot you are to waste good money on such a grand scheme, while enjoying a long weekend in the country. Can we start the tour now?"

Having refereed his two favourite people to a happy middle ground, Elliot squeezed Alice's hand to signal his support. To describe the house as a wreck was an understatement. It was an archetypal, distinctive black-and-white, half-timbered Tudor house which had certainly seen better days. The bottom half consisted of a crumbling stone wall, above which the second storey jutted out in a gravity-defying overhang. Framed with massive vertical timbers of oak and supported by blackened diagonal beams, the house's skeleton was filled in with flaky, mould-stained plaster.

The manor was exceptionally long, boasting three enormous stone chimneys, and it originally had two perpendicular extensions at either end to create an 'H'-shaped floor plan.

The wooden shutters, explained John, would have been a cumbersome later addition; such a sizeable house was undoubtedly owned by someone rich enough to have been able to afford glass, it was only the poor who resorted to shutters to conceal their windows. Many modern Tudor restorations had replaced the original roof with tiles, not least due to the potential fire risk, but the house that stood before them retained its classic steep-pitched thatched roof, replete with copious holes. John justified that although this original feature was more popular in the countryside, it was still quite a rarity and was one of the main reasons the house appealed to him, even though it would be a money pit to maintain.

The overbearing entrance consisted of a massive oak front door decorated with black metal studs the size of 50 pence pieces. Once through it, the guided tour took the visitors through an endless array of spacious, yet gloomy, rooms. The walls were lined with dark wood, which was oppressive, and the bright afternoon sunlight barely penetrated the grimy windows. There were lots of corridors, hidey holes and staircases weaved intricately throughout the main house, which only added to the feeling of chaos and disarray. Alice tried to follow John's instructions as he marched through the great hall, pointing out the original fireplaces which he said hadn't changed in 600 years, but all the rooms looked the same and lead straight onto each other so, before long, she found herself disorientated. She didn't say anything though for fear of being mocked, either for getting the directions to Cawston wrong or for a cheap sexist jibe about women lacking spatial awareness.

There wasn't a right angle in sight and the upper floor had a precarious camber at the overhang, which threatened to throw guests off balance and gave the impression the whole storey was on the verge of collapse. The scale was vast, both in terms of square footage and the quantity of rooms, and the trio were traipsing around for some time, overwhelmed by how much work needed to be done. After they had gone up one set of stairs and descended a different way, Alice was still trying to work out where on earth they were going to stay when she discovered John had steered them back to the start.

"So this is clearly a work in progress and not very inhabitable at the minute – that building over there is where you're staying," beamed John. "Your own little slice of history! Grab your stuff and I'll show you."

Behind the left flank of the house lay an older, and even more dilapidated structure, if that was possible; a shell of a barn to the untrained eye. The ancient building in which Elliot and Alice were expected to sleep, boasted the remnants of wattle walls daubed with mortar and whitewash, which had greyed with age and came off in chunks. The criss-cross timber beneath was clearly visible in parts, and horse hair poked out like an unkempt hairbrush. The wooden floor was rotten in parts and the window frames sported gaps where they came away from the wall. Inside it was crammed full of junk which had been cleared just enough at one end to shoe-horn in a bed.

At the other end of the room stood the remains of a primitive washing area.

This was what John had generously described to Elliot as the guest lodgings, which he could now only assume was meant as a joke. “John, seriously, how many rodents are we sharing with? It smells very funky in here, oh and wait a minute – it has its own ventilation!” he complained, spying the hole in the roof.

“It’s summer, you’ll be fine. Just be grateful I didn’t get you here in the winter.”

A scream broke the air. The men turned to find Alice spluttering and frantically swiping her hands across her face. “Spider’s web!” she managed in explanation, embarrassed by her outburst, evidently having walked head first into a sticky trap that was now invisibly clinging to her skin.

“Yes, sorry, lots of them around here,” admitted John, “but they do keep the flies down.”

Alice composed herself, but continued to pull imaginary strings from her fine features and check her top for errant eight-legged trespassers.

“I’ll leave you to get yourselves settled. When you’re ready, come and find me in the farmhouse kitchen, it’s one of the few rooms that is usable at the minute. I’ll rustle up a fairly simple dinner if that’s ok and then I suggest we all get an early night as we’ve got a big day ahead of us tomorrow.”

As John left, Alice gave her boyfriend an incredulous look and, with a heavy sigh, she mumbled that at least it was only for a couple of nights. Observing their accommodation with one last pained look, she put on a brave face which she promised herself would last until they were safely on the A12 home.

***

Elliot woke first the next morning and took in his surroundings from what had been a surprisingly comfortable bed…in amongst a junkyard in a decrepit building. As he lay slumbering, contemplating the weekend ahead, a busy spider caught his eye. Elliot watched intently as he – or perhaps it was a she arachnid – weaved across the dirty square window pane high above his head. It reminded him of a Jeff Stevenson song from the children's programme *Spider!* the lyrics of which were, "Try, try, try, but you're never going to catch that fly!" Before Elliot's thoughts drifted as to whether or not that was the spider's long-term goal, they were arrested by a lock of hair brushing his face as Alice lifted her head and kissed his cheek.

"Good morning, I wondered if you were ever going to wake up," he ventured, which was answered with the bash of a soft pillow across his head. Elliot could see the nightshirt that his girlfriend had worn to bed was open to the waist, revealing a flash of lightly-browned skin. Alice was very flat-chested so there was no heaving bosom to be exposed, but Elliot liked what he saw and slipped his hand into the opening and around her petite waist to pull her closer. She responded by wriggling closer to his athletic body and the inevitable happened, delaying breakfast by half an hour.

Afterwards, with towels wrapped protectively around their nakedness, the pair made their way through the jumble to the wash basin and makeshift shower. With no wall or door to protect their modesty, the pair were swift as they cleaned themselves in the wide open space. Alice prided herself on always being impeccably clean –

borderline OCD – and was torn between wanting to perform her morning ritual and not wanting to touch anything in the so-called bathroom as it was all covered in a thick layer of dust and dirt. The first splutters from the shower were distinctly brown with rust, but once the water ran hot and clear, Alice was in it washing off all traces that Elliot had ever touched her, scrubbing away with the same vigour as a miner who had been down a pit for a week.

Alice was also quite obsessed about hair, which was unhygienic and unnecessary in her opinion, so part of her showering regime was a once-over with the razor to remove anything that may have grown in the 24 hours since she last attacked it, leaving just a neat but very small triangle ("So I look like a grown woman," she explained). Elliot chuckled that it gave the impression of being a small dark arrow pointing downwards, just in case he was in any doubt where to go.

"What's the plan for today then?" she asked as they tiptoed their way back through the barn, careful to avoid the lumps of plaster strewn across the bare boards. Alice didn't ever feel the need to flaunt herself, so within minutes she had moisturised and dressed with the least of fuss or bother. Elliot would have preferred a little longer to admire her body, but approved more of her modesty than the flashy self-centred nature of his last girlfriend.

"Not sure really, I think we're in John's hands, whatever he needs help with. Though, to be honest, I'm not sure where you would start with this mess."

"I know, I thought it had been a bad dream till I woke up this morning and rediscovered the mess of this place."

When they arrived in the main house for breakfast Alice recoiled at the state of kitchen after last night's meal, and she quickly organised both it and their host. There was no B&B cliché of freshly-brewed coffee or the aroma of baked bread emanating from the oven; instead she made a pot of green tea while John fried eggs and bacon for the boys on a temperamental Aga. Being vegetarian, Alice herself opted for tea, toast and a banana.

"So, what's the plan for today then?" she reiterated, this time to John as she was eager to find out what was in store for them.

"The plan," replied her host over the scrape of the metal spatula against the frying pan, "is to clear the area around the building where you are staying–"

"So we can sleep in a carpet of debris to go with all the dust and plaster," muttered Alice.

"Don't worry, we'll put up plastic screens to protect the windows so the dirt doesn't get into your room. You see, it was converted into a storage barn later on, but the original building was about double the size and dates back to the early fifteenth century. It was a separate dwelling that probably would have housed the servants of the manor. This whole estate was once a huge medieval pile that would have been occupied by someone pretty grand."

"And now it's inhabited by an overweight, aging ex-barrister – ah, how the mighty have fallen," ribbed Elliot. In fact, John had been a successful criminal lawyer for many years; his sharp mind and an acute skill of being able to spot a chink in someone's armour made him a formidable opponent in the courtroom. At times, even the judges were intimidated by his forthright manner, booming oratory, and frighteningly-fast recall of an encyclopaedic memory. Having taken early retirement to write crime novels based on his own life – a rather bumptious, but successful move – he was now a best-selling author. The closest he had come to a court in the past few years was fighting the local County Council on a planning issue for his madcap project.

"Well that may well be the case, but at least it's all mine," John rebuffed.

A rumbling noise outside interrupted further friendly mud-slinging and a white flatbed lorry bounced its way up the uneven drive.

"That'll be Tom and his lads to lend some muscle to the proceedings," commented John. Leaning out the window, he yelled to the men, "Fancy a brew, guv'nor?" in his best cockney.

"You don't speak like that," Elliot pointed out.

"Ah, that's builders' speak," he replied with a wink, "You've got to use a language they understand."

Within ten minutes three people had become six, and five of them were devouring the bacon and egg sarnies John supplied. Wiping the grease from his mouth with the back of his hand, Tom produced some plans which he unravelled on the table, detailing exactly what they were going to do. Whilst he had the appearance of a typical builder – torn, dirty jeans, vest, muscular shoulders and arms like an orang-utan – he was evidently very well qualified for a considerate renovation.

"I did my masters in building history at Cambridge," he casually explained, in a well-spoken voice at odds with his façade. "It's a brilliant course, combining technical architectural study with practical building research, investigation and analysis. Rather than write papers or teach, I decided to use my knowledge to restore historic protected and listed buildings." The expression, 'Don't judge a book by its cover,' was never more apt. Alice found an instant connection with Tom and the pair were easily side-tracked as they swapped stories about the Oxbridge experience.

"Right then, let's get cracking," interrupted John, "I'm not paying you to sit here and chinwag." He peered over Tom's shoulder at the plans, which had a cup deftly placed at each corner of the immense sheet to stop it curling back on itself. "That's the barn you love birds are in," he continued, jabbing the drawing with his fat fingers, "and this is the part we're going to clear. Hopefully the guys have already put up plastic covering while you've been gassing so we can crack on."

It was set to be another beautiful, sunny day, but the early morning air had the sort of freshness about it as if the world had just cleaned its teeth. Wandering out into the garden, Alice was pleased to see the windows had indeed already been protected and began to view her accommodation in a new light thanks to Tom's expertise.

"The original building is from the early fifteenth century and you can still see part of the old footings here, covered with tons of soil, grass and bushes," said John eruditely.

"Do you know I couldn't have put it better myself," praised Tom, before adding with a smile, "well remembered." He continued, to save John any embarrassment, "We're going to clear all this area, leaving the older trees that are not in the footprint of the original building. I don't want to disturb these footings you can see on the GeoSurvey map." Tom was showing the plan to the newcomers, but Elliot and Alice just saw a bunch of squiggly lines roughly drawn on a blue paper. "We can probably use these as a guide to rebuild where the medieval house originally stood and convert the barn back to a dwelling, so that the two properties will eventually look something like this," he continued, pulling out another roll of plans from his bag.

“Wow, this will be an impressive looking place when it’s finished,” praised Elliot, glad to see something more tangible. “Far too good for you, John,” he shouted over to his mate.

“How much are you restoring it back to the Tudor house of the sixteenth century?” Alice asked of no one in particular.

“Pretty much all of it, but with central heating and a BOSE sound system,” answered John.

Tom herded the helpers out of the way of his men. “There’s probably not a great deal for you to do until the diggers have got rid of most of the debris and then hopefully we can start to see the extent of the work ahead of us.”

The noise was deafening as the diggers sprang into action; two giant monsters with the sophisticated touch of a gentle lover, caressing the soil and scraping away hundreds of years of foliage to reveal the remains of what had once been a red brick building.

“This is incredible,” said Elliot, fascinated to watch history being uncovered for the first time in hundreds of years. The skill of the digger operators was quite thrilling.

“Your guys could do surgery with that precision,” marvelled Alice.

“Wait a moment, that’s nothing,” boasted Tom. He waved his hand at one of the drivers Graham and jumped up into the cab to say something in the ear of the driver. “Watch this,” he said, pointing as the arm of the digger swung round to take the head off the top of a flower, leaving the stem untouched. “Now that’s skill,” he beamed and Graham is the best there is.

John ambled over to his friends, his nose in the plans. “I don’t have the map, so where do you propose the original road was Tom? Because it makes no sense – if the house was positioned this way round, then this current track appears to come into the side of the house." Tom agreed that there must have been another road to get into the village from the house, but that it had either disappeared over the years, or been deliberately rerouted at some point. "You're on a bit of a floodplain here, so that could be the reason, or perhaps there will be some clues on the old road when we find it."

With new revelations on a daily basis, it appeared as though John might have bitten off more than he could chew; he surveyed the area as a Matador would eye up the bull, assessing the situation to plan his attack.

Within a couple of hours, the area was unrecognisable from earlier that morning, as it was pared-down to a series of walls protruding out of the ground like budding plants in spring. "I guess this must be the original boundary of the building," observed John, "it's certainly big enough." The revealed room, measuring ten or twelve metres by six or eight metres, had almost doubled the footprint of the barn.

"Imagine doing this by hand," marvelled Elliot, "it would have taken forever!"

"They did have wheelbarrows in the 16th century, you know," teased Tom as they all admired the area, roughly half the size of a football pitch, which had been completely transformed from an overgrown derelict mess into a wide open space with potential. "That's a good job, well done," Tom said to his men, signalling a break from the hot and dusty site. The next steps are to get down on our hands and knees, have a look at the original footings and assess what we can salvage and what we are going to do with them."

“I think that lunch is due first,” suggested John and headed to the kitchen to rustle up more sustenance.

“I’m struggling to picture it – what would this have looked like, originally?” Elliot asked the expert.

“The medieval domestic plan was very much a transition in architecture during the sixteenth century,” Tom replied earnestly. “Many houses, particularly in Norfolk, retained big open halls until the early seventeenth century, however the conversion of traditional houses, by the insertion of brick chimney stacks and ceiling overhang, began early in the sixteenth century: an enclosed fireplace and a second story were being built from the first decade of the sixteenth century onwards.

“In terms of what the rooms would have been used for, this place probably follows the conventional medieval plan, allowing the private chamber to be maintained as a sitting room for the householder’s wife. This image is corroborated by numerous pieces of evidence which has survived in other properties, but the trouble is the number of unaltered whole houses remaining is virtually non-existent. Hopefully we can find something here – perhaps a brick inscribed with a date – which could suggest when it was built or converted. We’ll have to pick our way through the original brickwork anyway because there are often some interesting artefacts to be found. We need to ditch the heavy machinery in favour of our hands and brushes; it’s time to get down and dirty.”

Over a generous ploughman’s lunch provided by John, Elliot and Alice quizzed Tom on what life would have been like in the house originally.

“Tudor times were a vastly different experience, depending on whether or not you were rich or poor,” he explained, “but most things revolved around agriculture and land ownership either way. The majority of the population lived in the countryside and earned a living off the land."

"Yes, but the Tudor period saw enormous growth in cities such as London, Norwich and Bristol," interjected John, not wanting to be left out of the conversation.

"That's true, an increasing number of people moved to urban areas, but they were not very nice places – smelly, dirty and dangerous. There was no drainage system to speak of, so open sewers often ran down the middle of the narrow streets to the nearest river or well – which is exactly where the drinking water was collected from, it's no wonder disease used to spread like wildfire." Alice shuddered and pulled a face. "The average life expectancy was only about 35 or 40 years old," continued Tom.

"Living in the country was by far the more pleasant lifestyle, but as I said, it really depended on how wealthy you were. English trade flourished in Tudor times as tin, coal and lead were mined and the iron industry expanded, leading to a strong commercial footing. The middle and upper classes benefitted from an increasingly wealthy country, but while the population doubled from two to four million during the sixteenth century, half that number were still living in poverty."

"And when we talk about poverty in Tudor times," added John, "it meant that life was incredibly tough. They did hard manual labour for six days a week to have just enough money to buy sufficient food, clothes and shelter to survive. There was no surplus money for fun. If there was a bad harvest, plenty of poor would literally starve to death over the winter."

"That's right," Tom agreed, re-joining his original train of thought. "Law enforcement was severe. If you were poor, able-bodied and out of work, you were considered a vagabond and if you were caught you could be publicly flogged."

"What, just for not having a job?" questioned Elliot. "Didn't they have any form of welfare state?"

"They didn't exactly have the dole back then!" laughed Tom. "Previously the poor would've turned to the church, but of course good old Henry VIII tore down all the monasteries during the reformation and took away a valuable source of shelter for them."

"But what about this place?" asked Alice, coming back to her original question which still hadn't been answered.

"This was a grand house which would have been owned by someone quite wealthy. It is likely that he was a self-made man, perhaps a merchant, craftsman or yeoman, someone who worked for a living, but was successful enough to own property and land, and probably even employ people as well as having servants," suggested Tom. "Tudor England was very much about one-upmanship and you had to visibly show you were richer than your neighbours. Although these were residential homes, not fortresses, many properties boasted turrets, battlements and family crests as ostentatious displays of wealth. As well as building an enormous manor, you would also have to maintain an immaculate formal garden to show you were keeping up with the Joneses."

"How would the house have been decked out?" she probed.

"Sparsely. The furniture would have consisted of a few domineering, heavy, oak pieces such as a long table with a bench or stools – chairs were reserved for very wealthy or important people – and a sideboard. What else? A bed, for those who could afford more than a mattress, was usually a great big four poster affair. Everything was built to last and beds in particular were expected to be passed down through the generations.

"Tudors didn't particularly have carpets, but might have hung tapestries or rugs on the wall. Glass in windows was a sign of extreme opulence, most plates would have been earthenware and they ate with a knife, spoon and fingers – there were no forks."

"Wow," said Alice, absorbing the detail like a sponge. "What would they have eaten?" she asked, helping herself to a slither more of the strong cheddar John had provided.

"The wealthy, like the people who lived here, would've eaten a wide variety of food. They used the best cuts from all the usual cattle, plus more unusual meat such as badger, hedgehog and owl to create great feasts. The poor, on the other hand, were lucky to share a few rashers of bacon and relied mostly on offal if they wanted any meat. They usually ate rye or barley bread, and a hunter-gatherer diet consisting of vegetable soup, made from whatever they could harvest or forage, beans and, as I say, a little pork on occasion."

"Didn't I hear that all they drank was beer?" piped up Elliot, eager to be a part of the conversation.

"Pretty much," replied Tom.

"Cheers!" replied Elliot, raising his glass of lemonade for everyone to clink.

"Well, most water was contaminated by sewage, animal waste, soap and so on, so in fact it was far safer to process the water first and they ended up with alcohol. Yes, to answer your question, it was the most common drink and it was even taken with breakfast. Children used to have a weaker version or a cider."

"Good Lord," said Alice shaking her head. "I can't imagine what it must have been like. It's funny, I'm used to dealing with ancient history, thousands of years old, but I struggle to picture what life would've been like in this country only a few hundred years ago."

"Nothing much really changed during medieval times – say the fifth to the fifteenth century – but the Tudors marked the start of a period of rapid change, with the majority taking place in the nineteenth and twentieth centuries. You only need to look back at life after the Second World War to see how much we've moved on in the last 70 years."

"I know, when I was young we used to have to carry ten pence around for an emergency phone call, not be permanently attached to a mobile phone the size of my palm!" reminisced John.

"No internet, no computers, no email… life was much simpler back then," mused Alice. "There was a charming innocence of the time."

The conversation rapidly deteriorated into a barrage of boasts about how much better life was in their youth as they devoured the food in front of them. Having put the modern world to rights, John was eager to uncover more about his property. Tom divvied out the jobs and they all took off to different parts of the site to begin some labour-intensive excavation. Each worked quietly in his or her own section with a modicum of banter being exchanged, mostly about the searing heat.

"Elliot, John, Tom!" exclaimed Alice about an hour later. "Quick, come and look at this."

Tom was the first one over to her corner and saw she was holding what seemed to be a box wrapped in a piece of cloth. It wasn't heavy, about the same as a bag of sugar, which was Alice's way of measuring weights, and was around fifteen centimetres wide by eighteen centimetres long. Unwrapping the cloth carefully as the other two men appeared, Tom deduced it was a parchment casing. Alice felt it must be her imagination, but the pale cover almost imperceptibly changed to a dark brown colour in front of her eyes as it became exposed to the air. Underneath was a piece of leather, and inside that was a book.

The four people collectively held their breath as Tom gently prized open the fragile cover. Many of the pages were indecipherable as they were so decayed, but some were still legible. The sheets they could read were in another language, which Alice suggested looked like Latin. Barely visible, the bottom of one of the folios bore the remnants of a red wax seal.

"Wow," whispered Tom. "I don't know what this is, but sense it's important."

"Let me have a look," demanded John, eagerly snatching the find.

"Careful!" snapped Alice, who was still holding the parcel protectively like a baby.

"Yeah, we should stop touching it and wrap it back up for safe keeping," agreed Tom, without wishing to chastise his client. "We need to take this to someone who knows about these things. It might be something and nothing, but it's probably been here for a few hundred years so could reveal more about the house and all who lived in her. I have some contacts back at Cambridge still, so I can drop it off to them for analysis if you want?"

"Definitely," said John, nodding his head – he had skin thick as a rhino hide and hadn't realised he had been told off. "Where was it Alice, is there anything else?"

"It was here, wedged in this hole in the wall," she answered and they peered into the gap in the bricks – although it was clearly empty, they all strained to see if they could find anything else. Elliot tired of the futile search first and moved away. As he did, he noticed that there were two more similar recesses further along the wall. Without saying anything he clambered over the rubble to examine the nearest alcove, but it was just full of dust and cobwebs. Without much hope he moved onto the next bay and was excited to see another, similar-looking bundle.

"Hey, guys, come over here!" he yelled. "I found something else." Again, being careful as he released the package from its cave, Elliot unwrapped a piece of cloth to find a bunch of papers. These were loose leafs held together in a stack with a piece of twine tied around its length and width. Assuming they too were written in Latin, he handed them to Alice who was acting as official guardian of the past. Squinting at the faint penmanship, Alice concluded that they were in fact in old English.

"Really?" questioned Elliot. "I couldn't make head nor tail of it."

"To be fair, I am used to reading heads and tails," she quipped. "It's hard because the writing is very elaborate, things are spelt differently and 'f' is used instead of 's', but yeah, I think I can read most of it."

"Why don't you take both parcels to the kitchen and see what you can make of it all?" suggested John, simply cock-a-hoop with the finds.

Chapter Two

A Town of Good Reckoning

Most villages still have a pub near the church and Cawston's no different; The Horse & Jockey is just down the road from here.

The last of the summer light was finally beginning to fade when the three men came in from their excavation. It had been a long, hot day and, other than a few pit stops for refreshments, they had worked out in the sun well into the early evening, trying to uncover more clues about the house and establish the original perimeter.

Alice too had slaved away all that time, but instead of enjoying the glorious sunshine, she had been hunched over the solid oak kitchen table with the second lot of papers spread out in front of her.

"Hey Al, how're you doing?" Elliot asked as he lent in for a kiss.

"Weary," she said, rubbing her eyes hard and stretching her arms high over her head in a magnificent backbend, before crunching her head from side to side to release the tension in her neck. "This is fascinating stuff, but really hard work. I've been making notes as I go along, but I'm nowhere near finished. How did you guys get on? I didn't see you all afternoon, wow is that the time?" she asked, glancing at her watch.

"I know, it's late, it's the long summer days, they're deceptive aren't they?"

John appeared at the tail end of the conversation. "Look, we're all too knackered to cook, so why don't we go to the village pub and you can tell us all about what you've read while someone else produces a slap-up meal?"

"Sounds like a plan," said Alice through a stifled yawn.

"Tom, will you join us?" He nodded, too tired to speak.

Rather than drive down the long dirt track and back around to the village, the foursome crossed the field behind the house, clambered over a style and walked through North farm to find themselves next to the church.

"Aha, where there's a church, there's a pub," stated Elliot.

"What?" asked Alice with a quizzical look.

"It's true. I may not be the eminent historians you all are, but I know that most communities grew up around the two hubs of a place of worship and the watering hole. I bet you the pub we're going to is just round the corner."

"He's right," chuckled John. "Most villages still have a pub near the church and Cawston's no different; The Horse & Jockey is just down the road from here."

The garden area was busy, which was to be expected for a beautiful summer's evening, but there were a few tables free inside. The three men all quickly chose one of the generous fish dishes and gratefully took the load off their feet, while Alice stood and dithered over the extensive vegetarian menu.

"Come on Al, we're starving," pleaded Elliot.

"Sorry, I'm not used to having so much choice! OK, I'm done. Wait, no, I'm not sure."

"You have until I order to decide," he said, walking off to the bar to show he was serious.

Alice made a last minute decision to go for a wild mushroom risotto, then supped her cider as she sat down. "So, did you find anything more?" she asked about the rest of the dig when her boyfriend returned.

"Some interesting brickwork, but nothing that suggests when the original foundations were built or the full extent of the building," said Elliot a little disheartened.

Tom and John simultaneously jumped in to defend the value of the back-breaking work and explain the painstaking process of elimination that they were following. "We couldn't expect to uncover the full answer on the first day, but we're actually making great headway," confirmed Tom.

"But more importantly, what did you discover in that second lot of papers, Alice?" asked John, finding his second wind.

"Well, I don't know much about the period," she admitted, "so some things didn't make complete sense, but it looks like your house was owned by a man named George Sawer. I'm not sure what position he held in the community, but much of the paperwork referred to land disputes in Cawston, as far as I can tell. The writing is almost like minutes of the parish council meeting or something.

"It's all about the heath – apparently a character from a neighbouring village, Thomas Hyrne, gained the lease of the area and was suing Sawer, and a few others in Cawston, for killing his rabbits. Hyrne also accused the tenants of letting their sheep wander off the common onto the heath to graze, while they in turn said something about him increasing his fold-course. I got a bit lost at that stage to be honest."

While Alice was feeling a little useless, Tom was in raptures. "This is amazing, a real insight into what life was like in Tudor England!"

"What, suing each other over a few sheep and rabbits?" Alice queried.

"This is very typical of this area in those times," continued the expert, ignoring Alice's dismissive response. "Given the size and scale of the house, and the fact that he took a lead in the lawsuit, I would warrant that your man Sawer was part of the rising gentry." He looked around at the blank faces. "You see about half the population lived in abject poverty, but the other half included the gentry – landed gentlemen – merchants, yeomen and craftsmen. With hard work, success and ambition, a yeoman could buy himself a coat of arms and climb the social ladder to join the landed gentry. I wouldn't be surprised if this guy was in that category and owned a significant chunk of the land around the village, employing tenant farmers to ensure that he didn't have to do any work himself."

Tom checked that everyone was still keeping up with him. "OK, in a fold-course, the farmer moves his sheep through specific fields after the harvest, to graze on what is left and to fertilise the soil in return; it's a 'you scratch my back, I'll scratch yours' scenario. There were several problems of the time though and it only took one really bad harvest to put the poor at death's door and make them resort to stealing to survive."

"Rabbits for food," interrupted Alice triumphantly.

"Yes, indeed. And then the wealthy started enclosing common land preventing the poor from gathering firewood for fuel and tenant farmers from grazing their own cattle. It wasn't as simple as the rich against the poor, it was a case of villagers against outsiders, each man defending his right to a livelihood in a real cutthroat time. Do the papers say how it was resolved, Alice?"

"Um, from what I could understand it seemed that no one party was to blame and a compromise was reached. But there were other disputes with the same defendants a decade or so either side of the one I just described."

"What were they about?" asked John, the barrister in him lapping up the juicy details of a legal wrangling hundreds of years earlier.

"Anything and everything as far as I can see, a real litigious guy – religious practices, tithes and more land rights issues. It's interesting that you mention it was the village against outsiders, as I did get the impression that the people of Cawston were looking after their own." She referred to the notes that she had made. "There was mention that it had been a 'town of good reckoning', which had 'grown into great poverty so that those of Ability are scarce able to relieve the wants of the poorer sort.'"

"Wow," marvelled Tom, "this place sounds ahead of its time as the poor laws weren't passed until the very end of the sixteenth century, notably after a particularly bad harvest which left vast sections of the population literally starving to death." As if to make a point, the waitress came over at that moment with four plates groaning with food and the conversation paused as sauces were passed around the table and another round of drinks was ordered.

"What else did you find?" John asked once everyone was tucking into their well-deserved supper.

"There was some personal correspondence with his family," said Alice, in between mouthfuls. "There was a cute thank you card from his grandson, Francis Phelips, one Christmas." Again she referred to her note book which sat beside her main course. "In his neatest handwriting, he had scribed, 'Of all the tokens you sent I like best of the brawn and cheese and therefore send you most thanks for them, though the cheese be not yet come.'"

"He must have been reasonably well off if he could afford to send meat and cheese to his grandchildren for Christmas," commented John.

"Not very exciting a gift for a child though, is it?" she replied. "I don't know if it was a sign of the times or of Sawer himself, but everything I read was all very formal and business-like, even the family letters. His son, Edmund, lived in London and the pair kept in regular contact, but instead of discussing any personal details, information was reserved for affairs of the parish or capital city. It's all quite dull really."

"You might call it dull to read, but it tells us a lot about Sawer," interjected Tom. "I suspect he was a Puritan, devoted to both strict personal discipline and pernickety parish administration. The village status was an important source of identity for him and so he would have organised his neighbours to attend church and abide by the parish laws."

"Sounds like a barrel of laughs," mocked Elliot.

"Probably not, but it is likely he felt a great sense of responsibility that came with the privilege of wealth: he was administratively accountable for the village, as well as the self-appointed protector of local agricultural interests, while trying to keep abreast of events in the city. Did you see anything that named him as a churchwarden?"

"Yes, I think he was, he certainly had lots of records of who attended church and who was absent and why. You got the feel for who the troublemakers were, who was poor, who was ill and so on. He was either a real busy body or someone very influential in Cawston."

"Well, if he was wealthy, then yes he would have been influential," acknowledged Tom.

"Not much has changed in today's society then," remarked Elliot.

"Well, the poor in today's society at least gets a democratic say on things, whereas the Tudors had no alternate: their lives were governed by the rich and they were subject to harsh punishment if they dared to step out of line."

Elliot felt a bit embarrassed at being put in his place again, but John and Alice were oblivious, fascinated by Tom's in-depth knowledge. "If you had enough money that you had to pay poor rates, then you would have welcomed the fastidiousness of someone like Sawer," he continued, "and if you did not earn enough to pay rates, then you begrudgingly put up with the interference from the parish, on the understanding that you would be looked after if you fell on hard times. This sort of paternalistic behaviour is typical of the emerging Elizabethans."

Having been about to query something, Elliot had grown tired of being lectured and so changed the subject slightly to focus the conversation on the next day's tasks. Tom wouldn't be around over the weekend, so John was in charge of continuing the excavations outside. Meanwhile, Tom said he would drop off the Latin text with his colleague and be back on site on Monday. After paying, they set off back across the fields to the wreck of a house. As late as it was, it was not completely dark and they could still make out the footpath to avoid most of the cowpats. Tom picked up his van and left the three friends to the rest of their evening.

Elliot had been quiet on the walk back. Whether he was curious, confused or trying to catch out the expert, after a while he asked John, "Tom said that Sawer was typical of Elizabethans, but I thought we were talking about Tudors, as in Henry VIII?"

"Yeah, most people think of the notorious King Henry VIII and his collection of wives whenever the Tudors are mentioned," replied John. "Television historian David Starkey has made a whole career based upon the antics of one fat king, but in fact Henry was just the second in a succession of Tudor rulers from King Henry VII to Queen Elizabeth I. Admittedly, the two longest reigns were Henry VIII and Elizabeth I and, rather confusingly, the Elizabethans were also Tudors. It's a fascinating period." John hesitated, unsure of how much his friend genuinely wanted to hear. "If you're genuinely interested, I'd be happy to spell it out for you, but I don't want to bore you with a history lesson on your weekend off."

Elliot softened. He had been a bit rankled by being outdone by know-it-all Tom, but now in the company of his oldest mate, he realised he was keen to learn more about the period. He uncorked one of the bottles of good red wine he had brought, while John resurrected a selection of cheeses and crackers left over from lunch, and the trio settled down in the living room. John promised to keep the tale as short and concise as he could, but admitted he was riveted by the period and was prone to going off on one – he gave Elliot and Alice free reign to curtail him and keep him on track.

Chapter Three

Destiny and the Tudor Dynasty

By coercing parliament to pass various Acts of Succession to suit the situation of his latest fancy for a wife and queen, he lit the touch paper and retreated back into the annals of time.

"Does our destiny find us, or are we born to it?" posed John to his friends. "Is it an impossible challenge to try and change what is written for us in the stars?"

He went on to explain how the various suitors, detractors and sycophants who surrounded the royal court throughout English history had all had their lives moulded, and remoulded, by the tortured and tortuous whims of the royal head of state. Their fates were oft-fuelled by their own ambition to better themselves, their standing and the position of their families.

There was surely no better example than the debauched court of King Henry VIII. Jolly King Henry: self-obsessed, adventurous, a voracious appetite for life, a lusting for power and a powerful lust, blessed with a fine intellect that was ultimately undermined by his paucity of wisdom. Destined to be defined by his behaviour, it was his self-belief that he had a divine right to rule which dictated his actions.

School-book history tells us his legacy was the result of his misguided mission to produce a male heir, which in turn created havoc and gifted back-stabbing and social-climbing opportunities for those around him. The extent to which that notion is true is unknown, but we can be sure that the trail of lives bankrupted by his bidding continued to litter the pages of history books long after his oversized stature lost the battle to orchestrate his infamous tale.

Whether Henry either appreciated or cared that the future direction of the realm was set on a difficult path for many years after his death will never be known. But the truth is that he generated a foul wind of turbulence which would blow for many others, both innocent and implicated, for decades to come. By coercing parliament to pass various Acts of Succession to suit the situation of his latest fancy for a wife and queen, he lit the touch paper and retreated back into the annals of time.

His reign was littered with Acts of Parliament, passed merely to administer his whims. The whole reformation and split from the Catholic Church in Rome was devised to enable his first divorce. Then he brought in the First Succession Act, passed in March 1534, which removed Mary, the daughter of ex-queen Catherine of Aragon, from being a royal heir. Any reasonable person would consider the Act to be an insensitive gesture as it made Princess Elizabeth, daughter of his second queen, Anne, the heir presumptive by declaring his other daughter illegitimate. Even the good-natured Mary must have been affected by such a move, which was designed to hurt his former wife as much as his daughter.

The Act also required all subjects, if commanded, to swear an oath to recognise this Act, along with the king's supremacy. Anyone who refused to make such an undertaking was subject to a charge of treason, which was exactly what happened to Sir Thomas More. He refused the oath because it acknowledged the anti-papal powers of Parliament in matters of religion. More had been an important counsellor to Henry and, for three years toward the end of his life, had been Lord Chancellor.

More had also refused to attend the coronation of Anne Boleyn which, while was not technically an act of treason, clearly did not endear himself to his boss. Instead, More wrote to Henry to acknowledge Anne's position as queen, and express his wish for the king's happiness and his new wife's health, and for a while it looked as though he had escaped the king's wrath. However, More's non-attendance was widely interpreted as a snub against Anne, something to which King Henry VIII took exception. A variety of false charges were brought against More and although he successfully deflected the accusations, he found Henry was on a mission.

The king then asked him to appear before a commission and swear his allegiance to the Act of Succession in April 1534. More accepted Parliament's right to declare Anne as the legitimate Queen of England, but resolutely refused to take the oath of supremacy to the crown in the relationship between the royal kingdom and the church. Steadfastly sticking to the ancient teaching of papal supremacy, More publicly rejected Henry's annulment from Catherine. For good measure John Fisher, Bishop of Rochester, also snubbed the royal request and, four days later, they both found themselves residents of the Tower of London.

In July 1535, More was charged with high treason and tried before a panel of judges that included the new Lord Chancellor, as well as Anne Boleyn's father and uncle.

Unsurprisingly, More was found guilty and sentenced to be hung, drawn and quartered, which was the usual punishment for traitors who were not of nobility. Henry, in a rare act of compassion to his detractors, commuted this ruling to the swifter death of beheading.

Two years later the First Succession Act was altered by the Second Succession Act, which in turn also made his second child, Elizabeth, illegitimate, declaring her a bastard too. It is no surprise to learn that this change coincided with the end of the king's infatuation with Elizabeth's mother, Anne Boleyn, and followed her conviction and execution.

As a result, Henry was left without an heir until Prince Edward was born in 1537 to queen number three, Jane Seymour; the succession was subsequently changed by the Third Succession Act. This new ruling, passed by the Parliament of England in mid-1543, returned both Mary and Elizabeth to the line of the succession, behind Prince Edward and any of his own heirs.

After Margaret Tudor, Henry VIII's elder sister, married James IV of Scotland and became Margaret, Queen of Scots, her descendants were excluded from Henry VIII's will. Curiously, she was both the grandmother of Mary, Queen of Scots, and the great-grandmother of James VI of Scotland, who became James I of England when Elizabeth I died without an heir.

Henry VIII's younger sister, Mary Tudor, had been married at eighteen to the 52-year-old King of France, Louis XII. When Louis died, Mary secretly married Henry VIII's friend, Charles Brandon, Duke of Suffolk, and they had two surviving daughters: Lady Frances Brandon and Lady Eleanor Brandon. Frances had three surviving girls, including Lady Jane Grey, and Eleanor had one surviving daughter, Lady Margaret Clifford; Henry VIII's great-nieces. Henry's will stated that if the direct line should fail, the crown should pass to his niece Frances Brandon and then her daughters.

As King Henry VIII had no more legitimate children, at the time of the accession of his only son, Edward VI in 1547, the next ten people in line for the throne were all female. There were several interpretations of the order in which they should be ranked, but the names to note were as follows:

1. Mary Tudor; Henry VIII's eldest daughter from marriage to the Catholic Catherine of Aragon.

2. Elizabeth Tudor; Henry VIII's second daughter from marriage to the Protestant Anne Boleyn.

3. Mary Stuart, Queen of Scots; Henry VIII's Catholic great-niece via his eldest sister, Margaret Stewart, who had married James IV of Scotland.

4. Margaret Douglas; Henry VIII's Catholic niece by the second marriage of his eldest sister, Margaret Stewart, to Archibald Douglas. 5. Frances Grey; Henry VIII's niece by his younger sister Mary Tudor and Charles Brandon. Married Protestant Henry Grey, 1st Duke of Suffolk.

6. Lady Jane Grey; Frances Grey's eldest Protestant daughter.

7. Lady Katherine Grey; Frances Grey's second Protestant daughter. (She converted to Catholicism when she became Queen Mary's Lady of the Privy Chamber.)

8. Lady Mary Grey; Frances Grey's youngest Protestant daughter.

9. Lady Eleanor Brandon; Frances Grey's younger sister.

10. Lady Margaret Clifford, Eleanor Brandon's daughter.

***

John asked his friends to bear with him while he went off on a tangent to explain King Henry VIII's desire for a male heir, as he believed it was worth such merit given the influence on this slice of history. His diversion set the context of the experiences of King Henry VIII's nearest and dearest.

His father, King Henry VII, was the first Tudor king of England and founded the new reign, ending decades of nasty dynastic infighting among the York and Lancaster heirs of Edward III. Henry and his wife, Elizabeth of York, had seven children, but only four survived beyond childhood. The first, a boy named Arthur, died in his teens before his father; the second was a girl, Margaret; the third child, Henry, became heir to the throne; and the last child was another girl, Mary. Although the queen was in her thirties, the royal couple adopted the traditional theory of 'an heir and a spare', and so Elizabeth became pregnant again. Both mother and baby died of complications during childbirth. So, when Henry VII died, Henry VIII was left to sustain the fledgling Tudor dynasty alone.

The last time a female had been the remaining heir to the throne of England, years of civil war had followed and the lady in question, the Empress Matilda, was never herself crowned. Her son, Henry Plantagenet, finally ended the war and married Eleanor of Aquitaine to begin a new dynasty; the Plantagenets.

The dynasty of the Tudors was itself preceded by the actions of some attention-grabbing women prior to the action-packed reign of King Henry VIII. Catherine of Valois, who was wife of King Henry V of England and mother of Henry VI, committed the then-shocking act of secretly marrying after her husband's death. Her union with a Welsh squire, Owen Tudor, gave the Tudor dynasty its name. Margaret of Anjou was the wife of King Henry VI and took a very active role in the Wars of the Roses, defending the interests of the Lancastrian party on behalf of her husband, whose sanity was, by then, in question.

Margaret Beaufort married the eldest son of Catherine of Valois, Edmund, the Earl of Richmond, and bore only one child, Henry Tudor, later to become King Henry VII. Elizabeth of York was the wife of Henry VII, in an arranged marriage to end the War of the Roses: she was the last Yorkist heir (assuming that her brothers, known as the Princes in the Tower, were either dead or securely imprisoned forever), while he was the Lancastrian claimant to the throne.

"So, you see, it was very different to today where we have a reigning monarch with a strong line of succession behind her," concluded John. "Back then, childbirth was risky business, infants weren't guaranteed to reach adulthood and people died at a much younger age.

"No woman had held the crown in her own right and leaving only female heirs posed potential turmoil in the guise of marrying a foreign king – as was the case for Henry's eldest daughter, Queen Mary I – or remaining unmarried and childless – as was the case for his second daughter, Queen Elizabeth I. The Tudor line of succession was very vulnerable so it's possible to understand why he felt he needed to have a son."

"What happened then?" asked Alice. "I mean Henry VIII died thinking his son would take over and continue the family line, but didn't Edward die young?"

"This is what I meant about Henry lighting the touch paper and standing back. He had put in place a group of advisors to help Edward rule while he was still a child and, after much jostling for position, John Dudley became the young king's chief advisor. When Edward became ill, Dudley manipulated a new line of succession which once again by-passed Mary and Elizabeth, instead giving the crown to his daughter-in-law, Lady Jane Grey: Henry VIII's great-niece who had recently married Dudley's son."

"Wow, you weren't kidding about the mess Henry left behind!" stated Alice.

The drink had gone to Elliot's head and he was struggling to make sense of what he had heard. "I don't see how this Dudley chap can just suddenly decide to make his daughter-in-law queen – that doesn't seem fair," he slurred.

"Quite," replied John. "Mary didn't think so either, hence Lady Jane Grey was only queen for nine days. Mary's supporters rallied around her and declared her the rightful queen and poor old Jane was executed for her troubles."

"It sounds like the rich controlled the country and could do what they liked, regardless of rules. Much like today's politicians, hey?" Elliot contemplated refilling his glass, but was overruled by a wave of tiredness. He stood up, wobbled a little and announced he was going to bed. Alice, who had been drinking slower than the men, agreed it was late and led the way so that Elliot didn't trip on the uneven floor.

Chapter Four

Parish Administration

The harsh winter has taken its toll on the parish, though today's count holds fast, despite a death and no birth. The North girl was taken away, dead from consumption.

The sun rose early the next morning and shafts of light once again pierced through the holes in the roof of the barn where Elliot and Alice were staying. With a raging hangover Elliot was less enamoured with his surroundings, while his girlfriend was beginning to loosen up and enjoy the history of the place. Racing through her morning routine, Alice washed and dressed in minutes then cajoled Elliot from his slumber to join John at breakfast.

Like his friend, John too was suffering from over indulgence the night before and nursed a strong coffee as the pair entered the kitchen. "I blame you," he ribbed Elliot. "Something happens when we get together and I always end up feeling rough… how come you look so chipper this morning, Alice?"

"Ah, I was drinking water as well as the wine, and I wasn't guzzling at quite the same rate as you boys. I was thinking, if you two wanted to continue clearing the barn, I could carry on deciphering Sawer's papers – unless you want to have a crack at them John, they are yours after all?"

"No, no, you're fine. I think it would take me twice as long to decipher the scrawl. Besides, right now I am struggling to simply focus!"

"That's settled then," said Alice as she spread the papers all over the kitchen surfaces again.

"I take it you don't want any breakfast?" asked John. The lads tried to soak up some of their excess with a fry up, eaten off their laps as the table was otherwise occupied, and took a flask of coffee outside to revive them when the back-breaking work became too much. Alice didn't even notice when they left as she was engrossed in the tiny scrawl before her eyes.

When the trio reconvened at midday, both parties had made some intriguing discoveries. John and Elliot had unearthed some of the original boundary road and found that the plot was in fact quite a bit bigger than Tom suspected, which is why then hadn't found it the day before – they were looking several feet in the wrong direction. The friends bustled around the kitchen telling each other their news, Alice clearing some space on the table while John laid out lunch; a similar selection to the previous day's cold meats, cheeses and salads.

"Listen to this," she said as the other two helped themselves to food, ravenous from their morning's physical exertion. "Sawer notes: 'The harsh winter has taken its toll on the parish, though today's count holds fast, despite a death and no birth. The North girl was taken away, dead from consumption. Ill for so long, her passing should have been a blessing to the family, but I heard Mrs North wail for hours till I could stand it no more. I told her husband that she should mourn in a more appropriate manner for they were disturbing the tenants on my land. Overnight a carriage pulled up to the old keeper's cottage and a young lady has taken leave of the place. Yet to make her acquaintance, I am pleased to see the numbers remain even.'

"The man's a robot! A young girl dies and he tells her mum off for crying – what planet is he on?" Alice asked rhetorically, outraged by what she had read.

"Things were a lot more straightforward back then," replied John. "There was none of this touchy-feely HR bollocks we have now. If his job was to record the comings and goings of the parish, then that's what he did."

"I guess, but it still seems a bit brutal: you should mourn in a more appropriate manner."

Once the food had been polished off, they each resumed their activities, carefully peeling back the layers of history on the once-magnificent house. By the end of the day John and Elliot had cleared as much of the barn's perimeter as they were able, and Alice had systematically read and noted what she could about the comings and goings of Cawston, as reported by George Sawer.

John produced some Suffolk cider from the fridge as a reward for another long day and his friends gratefully accepted the refreshment. "At first Sawer was quite dismissive of the new resident," Alice said, apparently continuing her lunchtime conversation without pause. "Although I read on and it seems as though he became rather intrigued by the mystery lady. Listen to this, a day or two after she moved in he wrote: 'Having acquainted myself with the young lady in the keeper's cottage, I have found her to be a widow even though she is still youthful herself. I do not know if it is her state of mourning or her nature, but I find her to be rude and standoffish. I will persevere for it would serve her well to befriend me and live in harmony with the village.'"

"That's the pompous prat we've come to know and love," commented Elliot.

"Yeah, but then he begins to admire her. Another entry a few weeks later states: 'She has wisely sought my council on which vegetables to plant in her limited plot of land. I found her to be well-educated, learned and engaging in many topics, though she favours discussions of a religious nature most.'

"After that there are a few mentions of her, although interestingly he never uses her name. They meet regularly for 'theological discourse' and he says he is 'glad to have someone who is up to the challenge of a debate'. I can't find it now, but he is quite belittling of others in the parish who aren't capable of such a deliberation. He really is quite obnoxious and pretentious…"

"Ha!" exclaimed Elliot. "Sounds just like John here – perhaps you two share more than just the same house." Alice was uncomfortable at the insults that the two friends traded freely, but they both seemed happy in the knowledge that it was all in jest. Moving swiftly on, she read out more snippets from his records covering a wide variety of things that caught her interest.

13 July 1540

Mrs. Cobham died this morning trying to birth her fourth child. Funeral arrangements will be made for the following week, although Mr. Cobham does not have any money to pay for it.

Mr Hogg suffered a break in overnight, with the loss of a number of chickens. If only he had taken my advice and built a hogbog to house pigs with his chickens, he would not have this problem.

12 August 1540

Found Mr. Cobham drunk and disorderly in the towne tonight. Shoving me backwards, he accused me of killing his wife. He said that the actions of the landed gentry, myself included, were preventing the poor from earning a living. His slander is absurd. I am helping the poor, not hindering. I ordered him to wear the drunkard's cloak for the following day to teach him a lesson.

10 January 1541

Attended reports of another disturbance at the tavern last night, caused by Mr. Cobham who was inebriated once more. I ordered him to wear the drunkard's cloak again today and when he appeared sober and calm I warned him that his continued bad behaviour would not be tolerated. His erratic conduct is preventing him from holding down a steady job. He refuses to attend church; although his son comes to services, I think it is more for warmth and comfort than religion. I have refused any further parish help until Mr Cobham pulls himself together.

1 August 1541

The Cobham boy is now causing as much trouble as his father. I have had to caution them both this week: the boy for hi-jinks and the father for being a drunkard. Mr Cobham still refuses to attend church. He rarely has work and can barely feed his son. In the meantime, he lets the boy run riot.

25 October 1541

The winter has set in early this year and the sudden turn has claimed two lives: Mr. Grenville caught influenza and had no strength to fight, and the child of the Stewarts who was not yet two years old has perished. The parish records have been updated.

12 December 1543

The Bray family have been absent from church for the past two weeks. I stopped by to check on them and find their excuse. The eldest girl, Charlotte, is unwell, suffering from influenza – she is in our prayers for a swift recovery.

2 March 1544

Mr. Simnel died this morning. He has no family to pass his tenant farm on to, so I am burdened with clearing the house, selling his personal effects and finding a replacement. I have a mind to offer the opportunity to Mr. Cobham if he promises to renounce drink and return to church. The boy, William, would be old enough to help him work the land so it might also be lucrative for me.

15 October 1544

The harvest has been average this year, but the Cobham tenancy has proved a successful venture so I have allowed the father and son to continue on the land.

20 February 1547

Today we have celebrated the ascension of a new ruler – King Edward VI. We have had festivities in the village square to commemorate the event.

18 September 1548

The skirmishes over the land continue. Neighbouring landowners have followed my suit and fenced off their land in order to prevent peasants grazing their animals. While it is only right that we protect our property, I myself have had numerous battles over rights to the heath with nearby villages encroaching on our land. Young King Edward VI doesn't seem to be quashing the rising unrest.

20 June 1550

The annual sheep-shearing feast has taken place and saw the towne bustling with activity and celebration. A far cry from the rebellion of the summer past, during which we lost many of our men. I heard that Thomas Pole, the owner of the greatest number of sheep in the area, has invested in a loom to start weaving the wool he produces.

3 September 1551

Today the second Dudley, Nicholas, died of sweating sickness, less than a week after his brother Robert. His demise, along with Mrs Wydeville yesterday, pushes the number stricken with this epidemic above a century from our towne alone. This fresh wave has wiped out two nearby villages and I fear ours is heading the same way. I have advised our good townspeople to keep indoors where possible and stay well.

23 May 1552

We are to receive a new, updated Book of Common Prayer, edited by the Archbishop of Canterbury, for both daily use and to follow for Sunday worship. King Edward

VI's desire to maintain his father's Protestant religion rather than return to Catholicism is popular with me, but not universally within the area. Princess Mary and her papal tendencies have much support in East Anglia.

15 November 1552

Since the Poor Law Act was established earlier this year, we are required to officially record the number of poor in our Parish Register, so that the extent of the problem may be established nationwide. Of course I have been collecting this information for many a year, but now it is sanctioned by the king himself. We have also been advised to appoint two collectors of alms to assist myself as churchwarden to, "gently ask and demand of every man or woman what they, of their charity, will be contented to give weekly towards the relief of the poor".

19 March 1553

Prayers have been said for Eleanor North who is taken very ill with coughing, possibly consumption.

9 September 1553

Prayers have been said for the North family; not only is Eleanor still sick with consumption, but the cattle have murrain and must be slaughtered to prevent spread of the disease to the rest of the stock in the towne.

20 February 1554

The Cobham boy, William, who is now living in Norwich, made an invaluable introduction for Thomas Pole to a merchant in Norwich, for which he gives thanks. Perchance the boy has turned out better than his father.

18 May 1554

The keeper's cottage widow has started to attend church on Sundays. She sits on her own in the last pew, quite separate from the congregation, but I am pleased to see her appearance. She is fascinated by the beauty of the building and its origins, which is not surprising as St Agnes more than 100 years old and bewitches many who pay her a visit. I have taken the liberty of pointing out the great buttresses reaching to the top of the parapetless tower, the freestone and flint walls which are said to have been brought from northern France, the curious gargoyles and carvings, as well as educating her in the ways of our Parish. I hope in this way to gain her loyalty and perhaps friendship.

30 October 1555

A bad harvest is reported by all tenant farmers, and the North farm has fared no better. Many of our poor won't have enough money or food to see the winter through and our poor relief fund will not stretch to everyone. To add to the towne's troubles, Charlotte Stafford has just had a second child, which is another mouth to feed when the first is already so weak and they are penniless.

29 April 1556

Spring is finally here and I pray to God we have a decent harvest to come. Cawston's death toll has been high this winter after such a poor yield.

3 August 1556

While the townsfolk can only talk of harvests, I am pleased to be partaking of much more philosophical debates with the widow. I don't believe she has made many friends in Cawston, but perhaps, like me, she finds most of them beneath her. Thank goodness we have each other to maintain our mental acuity.

5 October 1556

Another bad harvest is reported. While the folk of Cawston have suffered, I am able to raise the prices of the food my land has managed to produce. Inflation and lack of available food is controlling the spiralling population, but I pray it does not continue.

7 April 1557

It seems as if Cawston is being besieged by an outbreak of influenza.

Alice pushed back in her seat, arched her back and cracked her neck in her familiar fashion to distance herself from a series of depressing entries. "Life was pretty tough back then I guess," she said wearily. "It seems as though every day was a constant battle against death – whether that's through childbirth, hunger, cold or illness. Many of their diseases could probably have been prevented with some basic hygiene."

"I don't know," interjected John, "the Tudors weren't as unhygienic as people often think. They did have crude animal fat based soaps and washed regularly. Henry VIII ordered several new bathrooms in his various palaces and residences, with taps and running water no less. It was more the fact that the doctors, or medicine men as they were known, were expensive and didn't really know how the body worked, what caused disease or how to cure it.

"Don't laugh, but doctors thought we were balanced by four 'humours', which were the different fluids in the body – blood, phlegm, choler or yellow bile, and melancholy or black bile. They believed that illness was caused when someone had too much of one of the humours. The so-called 'cures' were usually just as horrific as the disease, for instance if it was perceived that you had too much blood–"

"What?" interrupted Elliot. "Excuse me, but how can you have too much blood?"

"I know," sighed John, "but if that was your diagnosis, then you would have your blood drained, either through leeches, or by cutting a vein. Blood-letting was quite common back then."

"Which no doubt led to death, proving that you were sick with too much blood? They were barbaric!"

"And odd. Other 'remedies' included a heavy reliance on astrology to cure your ailments, 'medicines' to make you vomit to relieve symptoms, and various herbal concoctions for all manner of problems, including treating rheumatism by wearing the skin of a donkey, resolving jaundice with a seven-day dose of lice mixed with ale, and the more palatable prescription of goat's cheese with saffron for gout. Most of the illnesses were in the digestive system, due to the terrible water quality and slightly off meat, or respiratory problems, due to the damp overcrowded conditions and the ease with which airborne diseases spread."

Alice and Elliot were impressed and sickened by John's knowledge of medieval medicine. "Sorry, this is very much the period of history I have always been fascinated by and I guess I have a schoolboy memory for the gross things. If that had been me going through those papers, you wouldn't have seen me for days, but I'm glad you're the one reading them Alice, as I've got tons to be getting on with here."

"Hey, have you got internet here yet, John?"

"Of course – I barely have four walls or a roof, but I've got all the mod cons!"

"I'd really like to do a bit more research on the people I've been reading about, find out more of their story if that's ok with you? I've got my laptop with me, so perhaps tomorrow I could Google them?"

"By all means. Your boyfriend and I will just be slogging our guts out in the barn while you sit quietly in the corner, tapping away in the lap of luxury."

"Sorry, would you prefer I came outside and helped–"

"No, don't be daft, I was only joking. I'm thrilled that you're interested."

"So long as you're sure…"

When Alice and Elliot retired to their quarters she asked him if he thought it was really ok for her to research the next day, rather than helping out on the barn.

"Sure," he replied. "John's an easy-going guy, but he'd say if he wasn't happy."

"Well thank you. I hadn't realised how fascinating the Tudors were until Tom and John started telling us all about them. I mean, I had no idea that royal life was so complex and precarious, with everyone jostling for position as top dog. But then all that stuff I was reading about in Sawer's papers, it was like a different world again. The concerns of the rich and the poor couldn't have been further apart. And as for the poor woman who was queen for nine days, I mean that's just bonkers!" In her enthusiasm Alice hadn't noticed that Elliot had slipped into bed and was beginning to snore, exhausted from an honest day's hard work.

The next morning Alice was up bright and early again, eager to start her research. Elliot, on the other hand, was physically wrecked from the previous day and struggled to get out of bed. Stretching off his leg muscles, Alice giggled that Elliot looked as though he was preparing to run a marathon.

"It's crazy," he acknowledged, "I consider myself reasonably fit, I go to the gym several times a week and climb at the weekends, but a day's hard labour has killed me."

"You are fit," she said running her hands over his solid pecs and rock-hard abs, "but you know what it's like when you do something different, you're using your muscles in a new way. Do you think you'll be alright today?"

"Yeah, I'll have the water as hot as I can persuade that rust bucket shower to go, and I'll be fine once I get moving."

"OK, well I don't mind driving home tonight and then you can have a soak in a hot bath."

"Nice try, Al, but only I drive the beast," he chuckled.

When the couple entered the kitchen they found that John was equally sore and slow to rise. The two mates compared their war wounds from the previous day while Alice prepared the first of many pots of coffee to keep them going. Fussing around them to assuage her guilt, she cooked breakfast and did all the washing up before she got out her laptop and started surfing the internet.

Alice took some of the names mentioned in George Sawer's journal and did some further digging on them.

She started with the register of births, deaths and marriages, then tried a simple Google search and finally made some enquiries with the British Library on where else she could find out more information. Several hours later, the leg Alice had folded under her bottom began to protest that she had sat still for so long, engrossed in what she was revealing. Elliot came back to refill the coffee flask to find her hopping round the room repeatedly shouting, "Cramp!" by way of explanation. "Are you alright, Al?" he asked as he put the kettle on, perspiring from the heat as much as the physical activity.

"Yes, it's just cramp, ow! How's it going outside?"

"Great thanks. Hard work, but we are really seeing results. How's things in here, did you get the Wi-Fi to work?"

"Yes thanks. It's amazing what you can find out with the click of a few buttons."

"Great, I look forward to hearing all about it later on."

"I was thinking about going up to the parish church to have a look around the graveyard this afternoon, if that would be OK?"

"Of course, just take your phone with you. Not that you'll get any reception around here, mind."

Having been so dismissive about the Tudors initially, Alice was in her element burying herself in investigation. She had found out quite a bit about Cawston, which confirmed the information she had read in Sawer's papers, but the one person who eluded her was Sawer himself. She found burial records for a George Sawer on 30 October 1627, which she assumed to be the eldest son of the man whose record she was reading, otherwise he would have lived to almost one hundred years old, but nothing came up under the same name in the sixteenth century. She wondered if the church itself had any further records seeing as he had been so prominent in the congregation and a warden.

When Alice returned to the house in the late afternoon, she found Elliot and John collapsed at the kitchen table, dog-tired and barely able to move. Taking advantage of her captive audience, she regaled them of her day's discoveries. Thomas Pole, the man who invested in looms, went on to run his own business – Thomas Pole and Sons – in London, which was quite successful and ran for a number of generations. Unfortunately, the registered address was Cheapside, and the modest shop on the grandest street was razed to the ground in the Great Fire of London in 1666. Alice could find no further reference to Thomas Pole's woollen designs.

She found that Isaac Cobham, the drunkard whom Sawer had saved with a tenancy farm, had been a casualty of the Kett's Rebellion at Mousehold Heath in 1549. A total of fifteen other men from the town were known to have died in the skirmish, which claimed the lives of thousands. Alice found a reference to a William Cobham being executed at the Tower of London, but reasoned that it was unlikely to be the rascal she had been following in Sawer's papers as he had made it sound like the boy had turned his life around in Norwich. She could find no record of a William Cobham in either Cawston or Norwich.

The North family remained in Cawston for many generations and, after surviving a few bad harvests and cattle disease, the farm flourished once more. The matriarch of the family died not long after the eldest girl, for whom Alice had read that she mourned. The eldest boy, Robert, went on to become the mayor of Cawston and bought a respectable house locally. Two of the younger children died before teenage years and the remaining siblings stayed on the farm, working and raising their own families. The North farm still existed in name, but had long since changed ownership.

Charlotte Stafford, who Sawer noted as having a second child during a bad harvest year, went on to have a total of eight children according to the parish records. However, few of them survived infancy and only two made it through to adulthood. They all stayed within the parish, but she could find no further information other than marriages, births and deaths. Without any name to work with, Alice failed to find out any information about the mysterious widow of keeper's cottage, but she did delve into the histories of the pub which they had frequented and the nearby church, both of which were from around the same period.

When Alice had finished relating everything she had learnt, she saw that both men were stifling yawns.

"Come on Elliot, love, let's make a move. I think you might have to let me drive your precious car after all as I'm worried you'll fall asleep at the wheel."

"Yeah, sorry John, but I think we should best be on our way, we've both got work in the morning."

"Thank you very much for having us," said Alice. "I've genuinely enjoyed being here and immersing myself in the Tudors, and I can't wait to come again to see the progress you make."

"The pleasure was all mine," said John. "It's been lovely to meet you Alice, and thank you both for all your hard work. I'll keep you posted on what Tom says about those other papers you found."

"Hey, if they're worth anything, we'll want our finders' fee," teased Elliot before getting up and heading out to the car. He conceded that he could hardly keep his eyes open and let Alice drive his pride and joy. He doubtless would have been the worst back seat driver had he not fallen fast asleep before they'd even left Cawston. Although Alice had thoroughly enjoyed her historical weekend, she was looking forward to getting back to some home comforts and the benefits of the modern world, such as a power shower in a bathroom full of modern amenities.

Part II

Chapter Five

Thick as Thieves

Everyone ran. Rob and I were the first to break away and were just turning a corner when I heard Ellie scream.

Not exactly what you'd have called an easy life, mine. Scavenging, some would say. Sitting alone in the cold tower has afforded me time to reflect on a hard life cut short. I was born in a barn during the harvest of 1536 and named William after my grandfather. Generations of the Cobham family had lived in the village of Cawston, twelve miles up from Norwich and just off the main road to Holt in north Norfolk, but we were the last known survivors. The area was famous around the country for weaving, as well as the market on Saturdays and Wednesdays, but the majority of village life – mine included – revolved around agriculture.

You see, the parish had 3,500 acres, which was a lot bigger than the neighbouring settlements, and it included 1,000 acres of heath land. The farms were mostly arable; corn was grown in many areas, but then the sheep were herded over the fields after a harvest to fertilise the soil. The system worked well until other nearby farmers started to lay claims on the heath, to graze their sheep, put their cattle out to pasture or raise rabbits. The population was growing fast and resources were dwindling so, in a bid to protect their livelihoods, farmers started enclosing their holdings: this prevented us poorer folk from sharing the land, as was our right.

To say we were poor does not describe how destitute we were most of the time. My family barely made ends meet and we usually survived on one meal a day, consisting of grains and a few vegetables. Meat was a luxury I rarely even saw, let alone tasted, when I was growing up. My parents worked all hours of the day, and they sent me off to gather fuel from the heath to sell to wealthier residents as soon as I could walk and talk. Always covered in scratches and dirt, I was often chased off the common by other locals claiming I was trespassing. There I was, a small, dark-haired boy of five or six years old, hauling branches thicker than my skinny limbs from house to house, trying to make a farthing or two to help out.

My mum, Anne, had three more children after me: the first, a girl, was stillborn; the second, another girl, died after just a few weeks on this earth; and the third, a boy, died as he was being born, taking my mother with him. My dad, Isaac, became very angry after that. That was when he started drinking. He swore at God for taking my mother away and refused to go to church on Sundays for a few years. I still went regularly, to pray for my mum to return and for my dad to get better.

Dad aged so much in the months following my mother's death. He drank away what little money we had in the local tavern while I slept, then was too ill for any labour the following day. Frequently in trouble for being an argumentative drunk, my dad had regular run-ins with

George Sawer, the village busybody. The pompous, self-appointed local law enforcer made sure that my dad paid for his misdemeanours: if caught he was forced to wear the shameful drunkard's cloak as punishment while he sobered up. Sawer also kept threatening to kick us out of the village as the church no longer financially supported down-and-outs.

With the head of the household mainly unable to work, I had to fend for myself. Looking like the dishevelled street urchin I was, I soon learned to turn on the charm to get by: 'Kind Gentleladies, might I interest you in some of the finest firewood around?' I'd say with a winning smile. 'Lean in – it's so fresh you can still smell the moss. And when it burns, it gives off a warm light like no other which will make your beautiful faces glow. All this magic for just one farthing, you're robbing me blind!' Succumbing to a wink and a cheeky grin, the women took pity on me and bought a bundle or two.

'Sirs, I can see you are gents of impeccable taste, who accept nothing but the best,' I'd say earnestly to the men folk. 'And that is why I've sought you out, for this here is the finest firewood around. Handpicked by myself, this is none of your common kindling, but the youngest, softest pieces from the pines and poplars, which are perfect to start a roaring fire.' A little knowledge and a lot of bluff went a long way and the men paid handsomely for what they thought were unparalleled bundles of kindling.

For a few years we muddled on like this – Dad taking on casual labour whenever he could and drinking away most of his profits, while I made a penny or two to keep the wolves from our door. When I was about nine or ten, Sawer sent a messenger to summons us to his house. Dad panicked and gathered up the few belongings we had, ready to do a runner. He was convinced that Sawer was going to have him flogged or hanged in the square, but I argued that the messenger was just that, and not the Justice of the Peace. I reasoned that it was unlikely Sawer would risk us fleeing if he intended to have us publicly punished, and so it was on a hazy spring morning that we walked up to his imposing front door.

Of course we had all admired his manor from afar, but no one had been anywhere near it and certainly not over the threshold. As we walked up the long driveway, the gardeners emerged from the mist toiling away at the immaculate lawns and formal flowerbed. Personally I preferred a wild meadow to the regimented rows of buds, but Sawer was said to be caught in an absurd battle with the Howards in the neighbouring village over who boasted the best floral display.

Sawer's door looked ominously like a castle gate. I reached out and grasped the big brass knocker, rapping it against the solid oak several times. A man servant showed us through a large hall which housed a long table and several benches, into another enormous room where he told us to wait. Unsure of what to do, Dad stood awkwardly in the middle of the room while I inspected the furniture. The overbearing stone fireplace dominated the hall even though the logs on the hearth were not lit, and the heavy wood panelling around its perimeter bore coats of arms, which I assumed belonged to Sawer's family. Two upright wooden arm chairs flanked the fireplace and a tall, intricately carved unit stood against one wall. Fingering the handles, I was itching to open the doors to see what Sawer kept in such a cupboard, but I could feel Dad's eyes boring into the back of my head. Instead I ran my hands along the wooden panelling as I went around the edges of the room. Skirting a writing desk and chair, I stopped in front of an enormous tapestry that hung on the wall opposite the fire, admiring the craftsmanship that created such a masterpiece of a woodland scene.

"Leave it," my dad hissed as I picked up one corner, "and come here." Standing impatiently by his side, I stared at the many windows which were all filled with glass and wondered how rich Sawer must be to afford this huge house and fill it with such extravagant furnishings.

Sawer kept us waiting a while and then walked in carrying a whole load of papers. He deposited the bundle on the writing desk and motioned for us to sit on the bench, ready to do business. I fidgeted on the uncomfortable seat and wondered if we were supposed to say something, for Mr Sawer just sat and read his papers.

"Mr. Cobham," Sawer said after a while, without looking up, "do I understand that you are still looking for employment?"

"Yes sir, although I am a casual labourer and get work most days, so I'm not begging for charity nor nothing."

"And young Master Cobham, are you also seeking employ?"

"Yes sir, although I, too, have many odd jobs to earn money. We're not…"

"Very well, I have a proposition for you both: one of my tenant farmers didn't survive the bitter weather this winter and so I have a patch of land which needs tending. There is a hut over by the North farm that comes with the plot, and naturally you would sign the standard agreement covering commission on the produce that you yield from your area."

Dad and I looked at each other in disbelief, and then back at Sawer to make sure he wasn't being cruel and teasing us with such a lifeline.

"However, there is one condition," he continued, raising his head to be sure he had our attention. "And that is that you, Mr. Cobham, stop drinking and cease being a nuisance to the good people of Cawston."

Feeling the sting of Sawer's words, I witnessed my father's cheeks flush red with a potent mix of shame and anger. Not knowing what to say, he simply nodded his agreement.

"Splendid," confirmed Sawer. "If you would please make your mark here?" He proffered a document full of words that neither of us could read and motioned to the quill and ink well that sat on the writing desk. As Dad slowly placed a black cross at the bottom of the paper, we joined the ranks of the other tenant farmers in the back-breaking work which lined Sawer's pockets.

Although we both laboured six days a week, from sun up to sun down, from that day forward life improved. Come wind, rain, sun and snow we toiled the land and, on the whole, we made enough money to keep food on the table and clothes on our backs. Having a focus also seemed to help my dad get over his grief and he stopped drinking, as Sawer had dictated. Well, he drank less often and kept out of trouble, which he said was the same thing.

We made friends with the North family who owned the neighbouring farm; they were yeomen who had worked their way out of poverty and I think Dad was inspired by what they had achieved. As well as a few oxen for help with the arable farming, they kept other livestock and had a hogbog which stored the pigs and chickens, as well as a few sheep for both wool and milk.

The Norths had a lot of red-haired children, but the eldest two, Robert and Eleanor, were similar in age to me. When we weren't working on our respective farms, the three of us formed an impenetrable trio and became as thick as thieves. Rob was the eldest and not only the leader of the gang, but the brains behind it too, always thinking up some fresh trouble for us to get into or havoc to cause. Eleanor, or smelly Ellie as she was known, was the daredevil, always trying to prove that girls were just as tough as boys. Small, yet strong from working on the farm and eating well, there was nothing she wouldn't do. Rob would come up with these crazy ideas and Ellie would see them through with much bravado. Usually it was just pranks amongst ourselves, but sometimes it was at the expense of others, and that was when old man Sawer would intervene. It was never anything too serious, and certainly nothing he could ever prove, but it seemed as though it was his life mission to curb our high jinks.

That's where I came in – Rob and Ellie knew I had the gift of the gab, so if we were ever caught doing something we shouldn't, or found being somewhere forbidden, they would look to me to get us out of any punishment. My quick-thinking and bold lies worked in most situations, but if Sawer ever actually caught us he would increase the number of lashings for every untruth I told. I soon learnt when to keep quiet.

There was one time when I really had to upset Sawer to get us out of a pickle. There had been a hanging in the village square and the atmosphere afterwards was like a carnival with singing and dancing in the streets. Spotting a group of men watching a cock fight down an alley, I dragged Rob and Ellie to join in the fun and see who was winning. We were caught up in the excitement and stayed a few minutes too long when Sawer suddenly appeared.

Everyone ran. Rob and I were the first to break away and were just turning a corner when I heard Ellie scream.

"Rob! He's got Ellie," I shouted to my friend's back as he disappeared down a lane.

Sawer had managed to get one of his big arms around Ellie's tiny waist and hoisted her up so that her legs were dangling a foot off the ground. She shrieked and thrashed like a banshee, but he was too strong for her. Although she always wanted to prove she was as hard as nails, I could see she was petrified of what Sawer would do, not to mention what her father might say. I knew she wouldn't get a fair trial from Sawer and would get a whipping for simply being at the scene of the crime. I had no alternate to go back – it was my fault she was there after all.

"Leave her alone," I yelled at Sawer, running back up the hill. "She didn't do nothing, it was my fault we were there, not hers."

"That, I don't doubt, William," he replied, still holding onto Ellie and grabbing me by the scruff of my neck when I reached them. "But the fact remains that she was still there. I'll flog you both for attending an illegal activity."

I wouldn't let anyone hurt my smelly Ellie. Without thinking, I leant forward and bit the arm that trapped her and repeatedly kicked her captor hard on the shin at the same time. It did the trick: Sawer dropped Ellie and released his grip on me enough to wriggle free, then he stumbled and fell back with pain. Wasting no time, I took hold of Ellie's hand and dragged her away. We never let up our pace, even when we knew he'd given up the chase. We both ran the whole way back to the North farm and only stopped once we were in the lower field. Ellie collapsed to the ground in a heap, her body heaving with a mixture of fear, sobs and gasping for air. I was bent double, supporting my body with my hands on my knees trying to catch my breath.

"Th-thank you," Ellie managed to mumble as we both recovered from the sprint. Then she sat up and kissed me on the cheek. That day, the dynamic of our trio shifted: Ellie knew the extent of my allegiance, as well as her brother's desire to save his own skin. I made a promise to always protect her like the sister I never had.

As yeomen, the North family were comparatively well off. Ellie was always keen to point out that the likes of Sawer were much richer than her family, but I knew she was only trying to protect my feelings. They certainly lived a more comfortable lifestyle than Dad and I; they had a big house with some furniture, a selection of clothes and three meals a day. Because they had livestock, they also had cuts of meat for supper. Ellie would often sneak me some of her food. She'd meet me by the hay barn late at night and I remember it was during one such rendezvous that I first tasted bacon: I thought I had died and gone to heaven. A few years later my dad was given a pig in part payment for his crops, but until that day I had never known such tender meat.

I often thought we might end up together; Ellie and I. Of course I knew that first she would be matched to some rich old gent who still wanted an heir. She would bear a child or two then inherit his fortune and become a wealthy widow. That's when I planned to woo and marry her. I'd have built up our farm by then and be able to offer her a good lifestyle. We'd have lots of children and be happy together into our old age.

Then, in 1549, when I was thirteen, everything changed. The land disputes came to a head in the Kett's rebellion. The farmers of Norfolk, my dad and Mr North included, were so enraged by the landowners fencing off fields and woods that they rose in rebellion. Dad said I had to stay in Cawston and protect our smallholding, while he and Mr North marched to Norwich with thousands of other angry yeomen and labourers.

They demanded the end of enclosures and took control of the city, camping out on Mousehold Heath. Mr North later told me there was an attempt to crush the uprising, but the famers held strong. The Marquis of Northampton had entered Norwich with a limited army and fought the farmers in the streets, but they were forced to withdraw. The government then sent a much stronger force under the command of the Earl of Warwick to tackle the insurgence – this time the famers were driven out of Norwich. Withdrawing back to Mousehold Heath for a number of days, the farmers retreated west to Dussindale when the Earl's men attacked and routed them.

Mr North ran off and hid in the trees, but my old man fell in the charge and was trampled. His leg was broken and, along with many other rebels, he was caught and sentenced to the standard punishment for rebellion: hanging by the gallows. Mr North did not linger to see his comrade die, but came straight back to Cawston to break the news to me: I was an orphan.

With the uprising quashed, conditions in the village deteriorated as land became hot property. Mr Sawer said that he had no choice but to enclose his land to protect what was rightfully his. At the same time, he decided to change the use of my area to pasture for sheep as he had jumped on the wool bandwagon, having copied Mr Pole. Being evicted from our tenancy rendered me both a pauper and a vagrant, which was a criminal offence. For a while Mr North took me on as a labourer, but soon there was not enough work on his farm and he could no longer support me. No one else was hiring and, with Sawer on my back, Cawston had nothing left to offer.

Ne'er-do-wells were treated very severely: anyone roaming the city streets without a job could be flogged in the market place, before being returned to their home parish. The law that was passed two years earlier was stricter still, enabling long-term vagabonds to be made slaves. Scared and alone, I followed my father's last footsteps to Norwich. It was a large walled city, nearly as big as London someone had once told me, and many traders saw good fortune there. Hoping to smooth talk my way into a job, it was my last hope: I simply had to find employment, fast.

***

Norwich was like nothing I had ever seen before. Rather than farm houses set in acres of land and townhouses built around a market square as I had witnessed in Cawston, this town comprised of many narrow streets. As the population had grown, so the timber and thatched houses were built in a confusing maze, with second floor jetties virtually touching each other over the dirt walkways. Sewage and waste flowed freely down the street so you always had to be on your guard.

On my first morning, I saw an old man struggling through the street; he must have been nearly 50, if he was a day, and he was still trying to drag a cart of loaves to the market. Pretending I was walking the same direction on my way to work, I kindly offered to take the burden of his cart. He gratefully accepted and promised me a farthing if I would do the same every morning for the rest of the week. Flushed with success, I touted my muscles around the market place to women and the infirm. When I had exhausted all opportunities there, I headed to the tavern and asked if I could help clear tables. By the end of the week I had secured three part-time jobs and was feeling pretty pleased with myself, if exhausted. My day was just as long, and no less crippling than on the farm, but at least I was out of danger.

I had to get up early, before the sun most days, to run to the bake house and collect the bread in the morning. There's nothing better than the smell of baking dough, but it always made me so hungry. My stomach would tighten as I yearned to crack open the crusty loaf and let the fluffy insides melt on my tongue. I did it once and got caught. Old Mr. Shelton the baker, nearly had my guts for garters. He threatened to have me flogged in the town square, which was the common price to pay for stealing a loaf of bread, but took pity on me and gave me a hiding himself instead. He may have looked frail, but I was red raw by the time he'd finished with me. Still, he had to take me back on as he needed a dogsbody.

I hauled the loaded bread cart through the thoroughfares, delivering loaves to a few businesses. After that, it was back to the bake house to stock up for the market. Back-breaking work, and for nothing but a farthing, but I needed every penny. Then I would move on to help Mr. Bray on his fish stall. He got up even earlier than I did to bring herrings, mackerel and haddock fresh from the sea in Cromer. By the time his horse and cart arrived in the market in the afternoon, the fish was turning quite ripe and folks didn't like parting with good money on stinky fish. Bray liked my style: said I could talk anyone into anything. So I used to charm the ladies into buying his fish and he'd give me a half penny. I quite enjoyed it really, being paid to chat up the customers.

Then in the evening I helped out in the tavern – sweeping, clearing tables, watching the tallow candles didn't start a fire, whatever they needed. That sometimes went on late into the night, but it was worth it because I might get a few tips as well as my wage. If I was lucky, I could bring home two or three pennies a day. Of course, by the time I'd paid for my basic lodgings – a straw stuffed mattress on the earth floor in a dingy room shared with two brothers, John and Richard, a few years older than me – and some food, there was precious little left over. Still, at least I was surviving which was more than could be said for many others.

Mother had always taught me that no matter how poor we were, we should be thankful to have a roof over our head and some food in our bellies. Out of respect for her, and in thanks to Sawer who saved us, I continued to go to church on a Sunday morning alone in Norwich. Besides, the landlady expected me out of the house during the day and in the winter it gave me somewhere warm to hide. I used to have Sunday afternoons to myself, and that's when I missed Rob and Ellie. Mostly I'd go outside the city walls and lie on my back in one of the surrounding fields, staring up at the birds soaring overhead and wishing I was as free as them. I felt so caged by the drudgery of my existence.

I often thought about taking the long walk back to the village to see my friends, but Cawston was tainted forevermore. I had been forced out of the village that had been home to my family for generations through lack of work, harsh laws and a selfish land owner, and not even the ties of friendship could break through the bitterness that I felt.

Chapter Six

A New Life

The winter was always harshest as employment was scarce and food equally hard to come by. I undertook any work I could and ate whenever possible, near starving in between jobs.

And so I carved out a new life for myself in Norwich. I had moved on through an array of jobs since first arriving four years earlier – the worst of which had been cleaning the cess pits, and the most lucrative of which had been a long contract as a labourer for the weavers, which was a fast-growing business. The winter was always harshest as employment was scarce and food equally hard to come by. I undertook any work I could and ate whenever possible, near starving in between jobs.

Norwich was quite different to Cawston, but it was not long before I got used to the noise and smells. After surviving the first year, the dreary quiet of my old life held no appeal even though my new existence was fraught with danger. I had twice been mugged and witnessed several great fires ravage the city; in a matter of minutes, a simple knocked-over candle led to angry flames which leapt across the streets by way of the overhanging second storeys. Disease was also rife and if you were unlucky enough to have passed someone who was ill with the plague, you had to pray you were strong enough to survive. I certainly suffered my share of the bloody flux.

During sacred free time, John and Richard, the brothers I lived with, taught me draughts, but they were much better than me and usually won. In return, I introduced them to shove ha'penny, but we never had any money for gambling so it was just for fun. Another friend, Henry, would take us to watch cock fighting and suddenly, in the middle of the commotion, I would get a pang of longing for my old life. The memory of the fight, flight and sweet kiss of gratitude hit me with a pain I was unable to describe. I knew I couldn't go back, so I supressed it with sadness and continued to forge ahead with my new life.

The Candlemas Fair was held at the start of February, 1554; I remember it well. It was gone 5:30pm and night was fast drawing in by the time we had finished work. Henry and I ran down the road like frightened cattle on a stampede and could hardly breathe when we arrived at the market place – more than just an arena for trade, it was a huge public space which was used for pageantry, celebration announcements, public floggings, pilloryings or hangings.

That evening, all the stalls were open and lit with lamps, which attracted winter moths circling round them with a repetitious clink as they hit the side of the lantern. Pigeons were perched on top of the opposite building, on the watch for any food they could pinch. The crows were smarter and sat with one eye on the pigeons and the other on the stalls, constantly cawing. Everything was loud and noisy with the excitement of the Feast of Lights which heralded the midpoint of winter; spring was around the corner and hope was in the air.

We stood at the edge of the left-hand side track as people passed by, eager to try the exotic fare being touted: sugar, molasses, figs and prunes. We were not likely to come by any of these new products legitimately, for we had no means with which to pay for such things, but in the market place there were always opportunities to be taken if you applied a little wit and cunning. We observed everything to work out our best strategy. Many store holders had strong guards to watch their goods and they would instinctively knock you out, or at least drag you down one of the side alleys for a good beating, if they thought you were pilfering their wares. So you had to be sly.

First we walked by a seated woman in an old grey shawl, pulled tightly around her shoulders. She was sharing a plain mat with the vegetables she had laid out, from which she occasionally shooed unwanted insects. Next was the butcher who had hired a dozen different stalls and hung meats of all sorts on hooks – unprepared rabbits, straight from the field, pressed up against ones which had been skinned and looked like stretched baby birds. Whole pig sides, covered in flies, gently swung in the breeze as the butcher sliced off chunks to sell to an interested buyer. We were biding our time, waiting for the right moment to strike at the gold that was the exotic fruit.

"Boys!" someone hissed across the square.

We're no boys, I thought, me being seventeen by the day.

The urgent whisper came again: "Boys!"

Realising the insistent summons was aimed at me, I forewent the fruit in favour of the caller – such exchanges were often worthwhile, as the merchants might hand out a random job in return for a farthing.

"What is your business?" the first question was directed at me, again in a hushed tone.

I recoiled as the merchant's face was no more than a hand's width from my own and his breath tasted warm and stale.

"Don't back off, boy, I have something for you. How would you like some work in the city for a couple of days?"

"Down London?" I confirmed, unable to believe my luck.

"Aye, just some labour for you. You're not afraid of getting some muck under your nails, are you boy?"

I spread my fingers out wide in front of me and looked at the blackened ends which confirmed my work in a grate all week.

"I'm for that," I nodded to show my willing, "When?"

"Me too," chipped in my mucker, Henry.

"Sorry sonny, only one," the merchant replied.

"Both or nothing," I said, spurred on by the idea of an adventure. "What's the price?"

The merchant gave a throaty laugh and spluttered a bit while he regained his composure. "You don't even know what I want yet!"

"We've no food, nor money – so as long as it's not going to get us hanged, you can count on us."

"I'll give you a groat a day and a meal. I need you for two days, but it will take us two days to get to London… I'll give you a shilling and you can find your own way back," the merchant bargained. With only pain in Cawston and nothing holding me to Norwich, I relished the chance to go to London, so we all shook on the deal. Although I was paid handsomely for the work, now I'm paying the ultimate price.

***

Hopping onto the back of the merchant's cart, Henry and I hunkered down between his textiles and we left the square as the clock struck the hour. The trader clicked his tongue, but the horse was sluggish to move, weighed down by his heavy load. The journey to London was arduous and painful as we were jolted by every bump on the dirt tracks and cobbled streets alike. Because it was so slow-going, the merchant only stopped for a few hours' sleep and the meal we had been promised.

By the time we entered the gates of London, we were bruised and tired, but excited to see the capital city. It was indeed like Norwich, only bigger: just as dirty, smelly and noisy. Arriving at our destination, Henry and I stretched our weary bodies and climbed down from the cart. The merchant gave us an endless list of errands to earn our money and he worked us about eighteen hours a day. But, true to his word, he provided us with a hot meal, a lumpy mattress for the night, and at the end of the four days, a shilling a piece. We were giddy with so much money.

"Be careful boys, London ain't safe. You've gotta have your wits about you."

"Yeah, don't worry, we're used to taking care of ourselves," I replied nonchalantly.

"Not like this you don't," he warned. "It's different here, it's a dog-eat-dog world. There ain't much work and the poor make a living off robbing the rich, but they won't mind relieving another vagabond of his hard earned pennies."

With that ominous warning, he disappeared. Henry and I decided we would explore some of the great city before heading back to Norwich. The docks were bustling and ships of all sizes lined the banks of the River Thames. Wool was popular, and was the commodity that had brought our merchant to the city, but there were all manner of goods being traded, some of which I didn't even recognise. Ships arrived from locations all around the globe, and I heard people shouting at each other in many foreign tongues. The river had been frozen a month earlier and the Southwark bank still showed signs of where the water had been solid enough for skating.

We wandered through the streets up to the Exchange and saw all the wealthy bankers who set the prices of all the commodities. They were ripe for the picking and I began to understand the warnings we had been given. Rather than fleecing them – I was many things, but an outright thief I was not – we decided to make a few extra farthings by hiring ourselves out as link boys. We invested in two lanterns and sold our services to light the way for those brave enough to travel at night.

We stowed away in a warehouse overnight and were woken early as the first boats started to dock. We walked up and down the river bank scoring some casual work by day, and continued to help out the wealthy at night. After a few narrow escapes with the city's underbelly, we were just about ready to make our way back to Norwich when we bumped into two well-to-do gents.

"May I be of service to thee?" I asked, anticipating a negative answer.

"You're not local – from whence hail ye?" replied the older gentleman.

"No, sir, Cawston by Norwich."

"Are you strong enough to erect and take down a scaffolding lad?"

"Yes, of course," I said, flexing my muscles and slapping Henry heartily on the back to prove a point.

"If he can hold his tongue, he'll do," one said to the other, clearly satisfied with our strength. "There is to be a private execution on Tower Green tomorrow and we need extra labourers as we've lost some of our men to the plague."

I couldn't believe it. Back in Cawston, the village had gone mad over a public hanging, but I'd never in my life witnessed an execution. And a private one to boot, I wished I could tell Rob and Ellie. With the promise of a generous payment once the scaffold was dismantled – a whole shilling for a day's work! – we found lodging for the night and rose early with excitement.

Chapter Seven

A Secret Uncovered

I looked over to the structure where the lifeless body lay, slumped by the side of the block, the head lain by her side. The cloth that once covered her eyes, had been pulled off by the executioner when he held the head aloft. It lay by her side, somehow still completely clean, like a sleeping dove.

It was 12 February 1544; the day of the great execution. My mucker, Henry, and I got there early to erect the scaffold. We'd never seen anything like this before and watched in fascination as the people in front of us went through the final preparations.

Earwigging on a number of nearby conversations gave us the knowledge that public executions were normally held on Tower Hill with thousands of attendees, but this was a private affair to be held on Tower Green with just a handful of onlookers. The reason for the discretion, we were told, was because the victim was Lady Jane Grey. We looked blankly at our informant as the name meant nothing to us, but apparently she had been our queen for nine days.

The lady in question came onto the platform we had created and said to the crowd standing in front of her, "Good people, I am come hither to die, and by a law I am condemned to the same. The fact, indeed, against the Queen's highness was unlawful, and the consenting thereunto by me; but touching the procurement and desire thereof by me or on my behalf, I do wash my hands thereof, in innocence, before God, and the face of you, good Christian people, this day."[1]

Then she handed her gloves and handkerchief to the maid servant, who I was told was Mrs Tylney. The compact prayer book was passed to the man with her, who I later learned through questioning to be Thomas Brydges.

The lady slowly started to untie the fastenings of her cloak as the masked executioner stepped forward. She shrank back dramatically and said, in a voice loud enough for me to hear from my prime position, "Let me alone". We were so close we could see her hands shaking and could almost feel her breath.

Mrs Tylney helped to take off the lady's coat and passed her a neat band of white cloth to act as a blindfold when the time came. The executioner knelt before the Nine Days' Queen and asked for her forgiveness. He rose and towered over her, noticeably almost twice her height, and gestured for her to move towards the straw. Slowly, and with dignity, Lady Jane Grey walked as directed and startled when she saw the block for the first time, as previously it had been hidden from her view.

---

[1] Hanson, M. "The executions of Lady Jane Grey & Lord Guildford Dudley, 1554" http://englishhistory.net/tudor/executions-of-lady-jane-grey-lord-guildford-dudley/, February 8, 2015

"I pray you dispatch me quickly," she said as she raised the cloth to tie around her head, concealing her eyes. From our vantage point at the side of the scaffold, that was no more than one foot from the ground, we were right next to her. The poor lady was left for a moment, groping in her darkness and, like a child, cried, "What shall I do, where is it?" She staggered a few steps, with her arms outstretched, but no one came to her aid. Everyone on the platform seemed frozen. I leant forward and held her outstretched hand. Guiding her, I whispered, "Kneel here, my lady."

Blindfolded, she turned her head in my direction, so my face and hers were less than one arm's length away and for a brief moment I was caught by a terrible fright as I realised I was leading a lady to her death. But then something about her masked face caught my eye. I questioned what I saw – surely I had been mistaken? My stomach sank and a terrible sickness filled my body, to the extent that I thought my legs were going to give way beneath me. Breathing deeply, I forced myself to focus as I stepped back into the crowd once I had guided her hands to the block.

Glancing round as I took a few steps away from the edge of the scaffold, I saw that there was a small crowd gathered to see this historic execution.

"Lord, unto thy hands I commend my spirit."[2] Those were the last words from Lady Jane Grey as the axe fell.

My mouth was assaulted by the metallic taste of blood. My nose was flooded with the stench of bodily secretions. My eyes stung with emotion and my face, neck and clothes, were wet with warm viscous liquid. Crimson spatters not only covered me, but all those close by. A

---

[2] Britannia

flock of birds screeched overhead and jostled to perch on the high walls above. I was confused, overwhelmed and numbed by what I had just witnessed.

But still the ritual continued. The decapitated pate was raised and pronounced, “Here is the head of a traitor,” though there was little conviction among the public that Lady Jane Grey was anything more than an innocent pawn sacrificed as an example.

Blood continued to spurt from the neck opening of the corpse as the head was laid down by the executioner. The straw was saturated and red fluid ran off the edge of the scaffold to the grass below. I had previously seen the slaughter of animals, large beasts, but they did not seem to produce the same quantity of blood. This was quite the vilest thing I had ever seen.

The few ladies present in the audience were crying hysterically, and the gentlemen who bore witness were wiping the blood of this poor wretch from their clothes. The leaden sky and chilly wind were oppressive, and no one wanted to stay any longer than was necessary after having witnessed such a sordid affair. It appeared that people felt the quicker they moved away, the less likely the nightmare would lodge in their minds.

Wiping my face on the sleeve of my jacket only served to smear the blood further and I came over queasy once more. Retching hard, I brought up nothing but bile as I had not eaten in 24 hours. I sat a few paces away on the wall of the gaoler’s house to catch my breath. A lady came through the same door from which Lady Jane Grey had recently emerged, bearing a bowl of water and a cloth.

“You must clean yourself, then be on your way,” she instructed.

Grateful for the opportunity to remove some of the mess, I explained, “We are here to assist in the deconstruction of the scaffold, but that cannot be done until the body has been removed.”

I looked over to the structure where the lifeless body lay, slumped by the side of the block, the head lain by her side. Wetting the cloth, I cleaned my face, neck and hands, before passing it to my mucker. As the drama died down, curiosity got the better of me and I walked a couple of paces towards the slain woman. The cold weather had hastened the process of death; the heart stopped pumping and the skin took on a greyish hue as it seized in rigor mortis.

The cloth that once covered her eyes, had been pulled off by the executioner when he held the head aloft. It lay by her side, somehow still completely clean, like a sleeping dove. I could see the eyes were not quite shut, but half open. They were hazel and stared blankly ahead. The lady’s red hair had once been tied so neatly, but now covered part of her face. The image of her features haunted me, they seemed so familiar.

Those present were otherwise engaged, so I stepped closer still to absorb the mask of death, to see if I could understand it better. The head was lying on its right side in the straw. I looked closely at her left ear – there it was, I had not been mistaken.

Can a secret still be labelled as such if it is uncovered by innocent mistake? Is a secret only true if it is held solely by its originators? They, who are faithfully bound to it, are slaves to the knowledge that if one party divulges or betrays the confidence, the secret will be broken and lost forever. But what if a lady, a gentleman, a beggar, a thief, or a ne’er-do-well, by chance stumbles across such a secret – does that constitute a sacred trust as being broken? What if it was a secret so astounding, that merely the thought of it would leave the recipient stunned as if their breath had been sucked from their body?

Chapter Eight

Running Scared

The carcass of another beggar hung from a pole, the exposed entrails being blown gently against the wooden walls.

As soon as we had completed the job, I made my way back to Cawston as quickly as I could, to confirm or deny my worst fears. My mucker Henry was Norwich born-and-bred, so he wouldn't have known. Keeping my suspicions to myself, I replayed the scene over and again in my head. I couldn't get the sight of the axe slicing through her neck out of my mind, any more than the disfiguration of her left ear. Surely what I had seen had been a coincidence, a trick of the mind given the awful circumstance in which I had found myself?

Hitching rides with various merchants we left the city via Newgate, to the North West, and I was haunted by the decapitated heads hanging ominously from the archway – they were from unfortunates found guilty of crime and served as a warning to anyone thinking of straying off the righteous path. Crows sat on three crowns, pecking at the rotting flesh of the eye sockets with feverish intent. The carcass of another beggar hung from a pole, the exposed entrails being blown gently against the wooden walls.

Regular commuters to the city had become immune to these scare tactics and barely noticed them anymore, although the flies and smell in warmer weather were apparently a nuisance. We were not bothered by any odour as most limbs were blackened by frostbite, but the message remained loud and clear.

It took nearly three days for us to make our way back to Norwich. Without lodgings, any trip after dark was dangerous, so when dusk fell we left the road and sought refuge, somewhere safe to bed down for the night. There were many barns a short distance from the main track which often stored food so, as long as we were quiet and no one spotted us, we got both a meal and a bed for the night. The most hazardous part was coming across someone else who had already bagged the spot, as we had been told that vagabond travellers wouldn't hesitate to rob you blind, including the clothes off your back, before killing you if you were not nimble-footed. It wasn't uncommon to see a man who had been mugged in this way walking the back lanes totally naked. If the weather was warm a gentleman might stay in his birthday suit so as not to be robbed again – however, he then risked being beaten for indecency if discovered.

We were fortunate to avoid any such skirmishes as, even after some incidental costs, I still had most of my pennies from the merchant plus my share of the shilling earned that morning. Although my clothes were obviously poor and caked in dried blood, I was particularly wary and kept my money well-hidden, close to my chest.

Henry and I reached Norwich before lunch and parted ways; I told him I had some business back at home and would return in due course. I was tired and weary of wearing soiled garb, but in good spirits knowing that my journey was soon to be at an end. Beyond the city walls, I crossed the river at Hellesdon and continued on foot. It was ten miles across rugged land, which I calculated I could do in less than three hours. Emerging from the dense trees of Great Wood, I could just see the top of St Agnes' church. I was looking for the North farm, if it was still there. George North had stood shoulder-to-shoulder with my dad in the Kett's rebellion, but had been one of the lucky ones who managed to escape. He refused to talk about it when he returned. That was over five years ago and I had heard he had withdrawn completely ever since then, hardly speaking to anyone, almost to the point of being rude.

He still had a big family to support; four daughters and two sons – Robert, twenty, Eleanor, eighteen, Elizabeth, thirteen, Emily, eleven, Molly, nine, and Tom, eight. I had not heard much from Rob or Ellie since I moved to Norwich, but I often thought of them. News had reached me six months earlier that Ellie had not been well and I felt bad that I had not taken time out to visit her. According to the report I heard, for the past year or so she had suffered a coughing fever which had made her weak and repeatedly bring up blood.

As I neared the North farm, I was relieved to see George and his eldest son on the horizon, grateful that some things don't change. Shouting and waving my hands wildly over my head, I tried to get their attention as I ran towards them. Rob lifted his head first, shielded his hands from the low-hanging winter sun and looked over in my direction. Taking a moment to recognise me, he alerted his father, but the older man did not acknowledge me.

"Hello," I said, breathless from having charged down the hill.

"Greetings stranger," replied Rob warmly. "We don't see you much around here these days – to what do we owe this great honour? It must be three years at Christmas since you were last here. There's no work I'm afraid, if that's what you've come back for? You know I'd give it to you if I had some, but things have been tough the last few years."

"Don't worry, that's not why I'm here," I reassured him, suddenly at a loss of how to ask the question that had been burning on my lips since London. "How are things, how fares Ellie?"

Robert bowed his head and stole a glance at his father, who resolutely fixed his gaze on the grass in front of him. "You haven't heard? I'm afraid that the coughing got worse, she had consumption and nothing could be done. Eleanor passed away only a few days hence."

I felt faint as the blood drained from me.

"I'm vexed; I should have got word to you as I know you were enamoured with her. We did everything we could, but…" My friend trailed his sentence off as he couldn't bring himself to tell me the ugly truth again.

Robert stepped forward in a bid to catch me, but evidently was too late. I had fainted and found myself laying on the damp ground when I came around. Opening my eyes, I saw both Rob and his father peering at me.

"You alright, son?" Mr North finally spoke, concerned at my fall. "You gave your head a fair wallop when you went down – lucky for you, the recent rains gave you a soft landing." He and Rob held out their hands to help me up, and with their assistance I pulled myself to my feet. "Come back to the house and we'll make sure you're alright."

Trying to process everything I knew, I followed the North men back to their farm cottage. As we drew closer I saw the young girls of the household doing the laundry, soaking clothes in wooden tubs of lye. A single curl of smoke indicated that there was a fire in the house and I was overwhelmed by how cold and tired I was after my long journey. George's wife, Mabel, fussed over me at first, wrapping a heavy cloak around me while saying how nice it was to see me after so long. She asked what I was doing back in Cawston as she handed me a bowl of steaming hot mutton stew that had been sitting over the fire for the past few hours.

"I just got back from a few days in London," I said without thinking and watched Mabel stiffen. Wrapping my hands round the bowl, I sat back in the soft chair and tried to collect my thoughts. I didn't know how to broach the subject and was wary not to seem tactless by pushing the pain of their recent loss. But on the other hand, I had to know what happened. It all seemed too much of a coincidence; that Eleanor had passed so suddenly, given what I had seen in London.

Turning to my friend, I tried what I thought was a subtle approach: "Rob, do you remember when you, Ellie and I were playing in the big old oak tree when we were little? Ellie must have been a young girl still. We managed to get three-quarters of the way up and you dared Ellie to go all the way to the top. She was so close when she slipped and fell through the branches down to the ground. By the time we had clambered down, she was covered in blood and we were petrified at what damage she had done. Thank God it was just her left ear lobe which had been caught and ripped clean off. Poor Ellie, she never wore her hair tied back after that, she was so self-conscious about her missing lobe. I preferred it when wore her locks loose anyway."

Robert smiled, lost briefly in the memory, then changed the subject, "Yeah, the old oak came down in the big storm a few years back; provided enough firewood to keep us warm all winter." While Robert carried on regaling stories of the harsh weather and the struggles they had been through, Mabel became very agitated and the atmosphere in the room turned tense and uncomfortable.

"We're all still very upset," said George, breaking the silence that had descended, "so I think it's best you leave now. Perchance, stay away for a bit; you remind us too much of our beloved Eleanor. I imagine you're busy enough anyway, so prithy don't return until it's harvest time – we'll see if we can get you work then."

I couldn't really complain as I hadn't visited since I left their farm when things became tough, but I still wanted answers. "George, where is Eleanor buried? I would like to go and say farewell, pay my respects." Now the colour drained from George's face and I thought it would be me picking him up off the ground.

"You- you can't," he stammered. "I did it in an unmarked spot where no one knows – that's what Mabel wanted, so prithy do not ask again." With that, he grabbed my hand and said, "See you around, son. I know you were close with Eleanor, but please forget about her and move on."

***

Promising that I would leave them in peace, I turned and began the long walk home. Dusk was enveloping the land around me and I didn't fancy my chances alone on the road overnight. I began looking for a place to sleep when I spied someone trundling towards me in a cart. Recognising a face familiar from my past in the driver's seat, I stepped out as he approached.

"Hail, William Cobham, as I live and breathe!" exclaimed Thomas Pole, pulling his horse to a halt. "How farest thou?"

"I fare well, and thee. Wither goest thou at such an hour?"

"I'm hoping for some trade in Norwich first thing in the morning so I wanted to arrive with time to find lodgings for the night, but fear I'm too late already. I'd be happy to hear your news, but don't care to linger any longer than necessary."

"This bodes well; I hail from Norwich now – mayest I be of service to thee? For the offer of a ride, I could fix you up with lodgings, what sayest thou?"

"Pray sit ye down!" he said, gesturing to the bench he occupied. As I settled myself beside Thomas on the hard wooden seat he signalled for the horse to walk on. The cart rumbled forward, gently at first and then roughly as it gained pace.

"What wares are you offering in Norwich?" I asked.

"We invested in sheep a few years ago and have been building up a business on the wool that we get from them. We've got some beauteous woollen garments for sale to keep the good folk of Norwich warm until spring comes round."

"Ingenious Thomas. Tell me, are you seeking a stall yourself or are you looking to sell wholesale?"

"I'd rather find a wholesaler than try my luck on the market all day, only to come home with the same stock."

"I might know someone who can help, if you want me to make introductions?"

"That would be most kind. It is hap'ly that we met this evening."

"So what of Cawston is my absence, prithy avail me of the news?" I asked with a plan in mind.

"Been a tough few years, but nowt much has changed. Sawer's still arguing with neighbouring villages over land. The Shore girl, Charlotte, was betrothed to Mr Stafford and is with child. Both the Dudley boys got the sweating sickness and passed. The market continues, as does the tavern. There was some disease on the North farm last year, they were forced to slaughter their cattle so as not to contaminate other beasts. It crippled George–"

"What about Eleanor North, I heard she was sick?"

"Poor thing, been coughing since last winter, never seemed to be able to rid herself of it. They suspected consumption and I heard tales that she had gone to London to visit an apothecary, but it was too late."

Thomas had spoken enough; my worst fears were confirmed and a chill ran down my spine. Somehow, the lady I had helped to the executioner's block had been my beloved Eleanor. I vowed to uncover whatever dark plot lay behind the tragedy.

As the cart rattled through the gates into Norwich I remembered my promise to help Thomas secure a wholesaler for his wool, but resolved that afterwards I would return to London to find some answers. Sure in my mind that somehow it had happened, I was perplexed over the possibility and curious to learn the details. Back in the city I now called home, I directed Thomas to a nearby tavern which I knew my contact frequented. Thomas purchased us a welcome ale each while I scanned the crowd for the ruddy face I sought.

Clearly uncomfortable in the big city, Thomas confided that he felt very fortunate to have bumped into me. Conversely, I had forgotten how insular life had been back in Cawston and was relieved to have had a swift passage back to the more anonymous existence I presently led. In the village, I had never been allowed to forget the debt my dad and I owed to Sawer, and he held it as a silent threat over my head every day while I was growing up.

In a dark corner I spied Mr Dormer, the large wealthy merchant I believed would be interested in Thomas' woollen garb, and, true to my word, I strode over to him and made the necessary introductions.

"Mr Dormer, sir, you are in luck," I said brazenly, "for I bumped into this fine fellow today. I have not seen him in many a year, but have heard good things from the folks of Cawston about his excellent work. You should be blessed to have the opportunity of representing his expert craft here in this fine city of Norwich."

"What is it William?" he asked eagerly, his ruddy cheeks flushing with excitement. "You have failed to tell me the craft in which this gentleman is supposed to excel."

"Why, wool, of course – this man is none other than Thomas Pole. I am sure that you too have heard of him, any merchant worth his salt in the south east is aware of his designs." High on the power of such a shameless sale, I continued to boast of the fine quality of Thomas' work even though I had never seen it myself. I even began personally vouching for the success that Mr Dormer would undoubtedly achieve in the market with such exceptional goods. Thomas looked at me with his eyes wide and mouth agape, but I maintained my bold stance. I wondered how much of my bravado relied on the fact that I intended to be on my way to London by the time Mr Dormer could test my claims.

"Yes, I think I have heard of Mr Pole," stammered the merchant, trying to save face. "Pleased to meet you sir and it would indeed be a privilege for me to sell your wares for you. What be thy pleasure?" With that Mr Dormer raised his bulk to shake hands and order another round of ale, before the pair sat to discuss the finer details of cost and quantity.

Pleased that I had done a good deed, I excused myself to plan my next steps to find out the truth about Ellie. Scanning the tavern, I recognised some faces, but there were plenty who I judged to be passing through. These were the ones I approached to see if I might hitch a lift to London.

"What taketh you back there so soon?" a familiar voice asked from behind me, and I spun round to see my old mucker.

"Henry! Good day to you again. How has your afternoon fared?"

"Not good, there's no work to be had. That's why I was curious as to why you were going back to London – thought I might join you as there's nowt here for me."

"No work for me either I'm afraid; just some personal business."

"What about if we went together and rustled up some work like last time? That scaffolding job paid well, we could see if there were any more executions scheduled. Or perhaps they need labourers to prepare the stakes as I hear Bloody Mary is burning ardent Protestants apace now she is converting the country back to Catholicism?"

"Sorry Henry, this is something that I've got to do on my own."

"What, like the business you had back in Cawston, when you brought a wool trader back and introduced him to Dormer? I'm nobody's fool William Cobham, I'm sure you'll be paid handsomely for that," he said spitefully, "you just don't want to share the shillings. And after all I've done for you–"

"Henry, hold your tongue. I brought you along for the job in London, remember? I've always looked out for you, we're like brothers. What are you talking about?"

"Well I thought we were like brothers, but then you ran off to Cawston to make your fortune and left me to fend for myself."

"Sorry Henry, but it wasn't like that. I didn't go to see Mr Pole – that really was just a fortuitous meeting on my return journey – I went back to Cawston because of something we saw in London, something from my past."

"I'm listening," said Henry, less angry now, more intrigued.

"I can't... I shouldn't... really, I can't say."

"William," he said, placing his hand on my shoulder, "I'm your brother, remember? You can tell me anything."

In truth, what I had seen and heard had been eating me up for days and I was no further forward in my plans, so I decided to confide in Henry to see if he had any ideas. When I had finished explaining everything I knew about Lady Jane Grey's double, he let out a long low whistle. "That's a pickle for sure, what are you going to do?"

"I really don't know Henry, but I know I have to get to London to find out what happened."

"Then I'm definitely coming with you, brother. You know as well as I that it's not a safe city, I can be your guard. And it sounds like you could benefit from some help finding your Ellie."

Henry was right: London did scare me and having a big chap for protection probably wouldn't hurt. Besides, he was good company and might well aid me uncover the facts. "I thank you heartily, now what is your pleasure?"

Over another ale we spoke to more travellers and finally found someone willing to give us both a ride to London. We made plans to meet in the morning and then I retrieved Thomas who was grateful to spend the night in my humble lodgings. My friend fell into a deep and sound sleep, snoring next to me on my mattress. In contrast I was restless, my mind plagued by images of the most beautiful face and a damaged ear. As dawn broke, both Thomas and I prepared to leave Norwich: he, content and bound for Cawston; me, agitated and destined for London with my mucker Henry.

Chapter Nine

Breaking into the Tower

The cart rumbled through Newgate and my insides lurched as I spied the portentous decaying limbs welcoming us back to the city.

Henry and I squeezed into the back of a cart fully laden with textiles bound for foreign shores via the docks on the River Thames. I spent much of my time on the jarring journey to the capital trying to unravel the information I held: Eleanor was dead, having possibly travelled to an apothecary in London, while the queen I had seen executed, impossibly appeared to have the same childhood scar I knew first hand. As London loomed in the distance, I felt my stomach tighten with both hunger and anticipation. The cart rumbled through Newgate and my insides lurched as I spied the portentous decaying limbs welcoming us back to the city.

Unsure how the two events could be connected, I had no idea what I was going to do or how I would find the information I so keenly sought when we bade farewell to the merchant at the docks. Presently I was grateful to have Henry's company as he remembered the city's layout better than I, and led us through the narrow, dirty, smelly streets back to the Tower of London. Hanging around the postern gate, we hoped to recognise someone from the fateful day a week hence. It took many hours, but eventually I saw a woman return from market laden with goods, and knew her to be the one who helped clean the blood off me.

"Hail! Wilt thou attend me?" I greeted her warmly, but she pushed past me and continued on her way.

"My name is William; we were the labourers hired to take care of the scaffold the other day."

Still no answer.

"What of the head and body of the lady executed here that day?"

"What of it, lad?"

"I wondered if I might be able to pay my last respects and see the lady once more?"

"No."

The old woman's face was set in stone and her steely eyes warned me she meant business, but with no other leads to pursue, I felt I had no choice.

"I think I recognised her–"

"Of course you did. Lady Jane Grey claimed to be the queen of England for a brief period, any fool knows that!"

"Actually, I thought–"

"Well whatever you thought, you're too late. Your Queen of Nine Days has been buried already in the Chapel of St Peter ad Vincula on the north side of Tower Green."

"What if told you that I thought I saw a secret? Something which no one else knows, but a secret which could rock the foundations of the current queen's reign?"

"Then I'd warn you again to keep your lips sealed or be branded a traitor."

"But if I could just see her head again, I could prove it."

"Like I said, you're too late: she's dead and buried. What do you want to do about it – dig her up?" the old woman barked, her ire growing fast. "You kids, you're a macabre lot." She sent me off with a flea in my ear and shuffled through the postern gate. Frustrated, I turned to Henry to ask what next.

"Food," he announced, "I'm starving."

The angst of the day ebbed and I too discovered I was ravenous. Settling down at a nearby tavern, we discussed our options over an ale and bowl of stew.

"Without that head, you've got no proof," Henry said, most unhelpfully.

"But if she's been buried already, there's not much we can do," I reasoned. "How feasible do you think it would be to dig up the grave, supposedly of Lady Jane Grey? I mean it would still be fresh – we could buy some tools and it would be back-breaking work, but between us it shouldn't take too long. Of course, there is the not insignificant issue of actually gaining entrance to the cemetery, perchance a disguise might be required?"

It wasn't much of a plan, but it was all we had. We agreed to undertake some reconnaissance work before we tried to steal the body and returned once more to the Tower. Walking around the imposing fortress, we had no idea how we might scale the high walls in order to break into the inner sanctum, find the chapel and reveal the truth about Eleanor. Stopping at one corner where the moat was at its narrowest I surveyed a sprawling old oak tree; it stood wide and proud, its branches far reaching. An expert tree climber, I wondered if I might be able to use it to get onto the outer walls. Instinctively I started climbing, while Henry remained rooted to the spot. Looking up at me with confusion as I began jumping from branch to branch like a squirrel, he hissed, “Psst! William, what the devil are you doing?”

“Have patience… you’ll see.”

Reaching one of the thickest, longest branches, I lay flat spreading my weight along its length. Edging out further away from the trunk and towards the royal walls, I held my breath. I heard the bough creak, like ice on a lake, and knew I didn’t have long. Grabbing the limb firmly with both hands I used my body like a pendulum, swinging back and forth to gain momentum. Just as I intended to let go and jump down onto the walls, there was a loud crack and the wood gave way. I fell to the earth and let out an involuntary wail as I hit the hard ground.

“William! Are you OK? What on earth were you thinking?”

“My ankle,” I cried as I held it and rolled around in agony.

“Shhh, you’ll attract attention,” reprimanded Henry, too late.

“You there, what’s going on?” shouted a burly guard, disturbed by the commotion. He started running towards us as fast as his armour would allow. Henry tried to pull me up, but I couldn’t put any weight on my left leg and was rendered useless.

“Run,” I told him, but my faithful mucker refused to leave my side. To the hollers of the guard closing in on us, Henry hoisted me onto his square shoulders and attempted to carry me to safety. But the guard gave chase and presently caught us.

"What were you lads doing in that oak tree?"

"Nothing sir, just playing," I said innocently, hopefully. "Didn't you ever climb a tree?"

"Not since I was a boy, but a word of advice: don't climb trees round the tower or you'll lose your head." He drew his hand across his neck simulating a beheading.

"I know, we did the scaffolding for the recent execution – the one for Lady Jane Grey," I said, noting that I had his interest. "Blood everywhere! Did you see it?"

"I was on duty round the other side, but I heard all about it. Someone said it took ten swings of the axe to severe her head and it was a complete farce."

"Ten swings of the axe? You've been fooled, good sir, it was just one clean sweep. We know, we were right there."

"Are you calling me a liar?"

"No sir, just misinformed. If you let me dig up the body, I'll prove it to you, for the cut is orderly."

"Now it is you who is misinformed," the guard said triumphantly. "Lady Jane Grey lies in waiting in the crypt, she is due to be buried at the weekend." My eyes widened with the news and my mind raced into planning mode, though my ankle throbbed in pain.

"Then, pray sir, accompany us to the crypt and I will prove you were told a tale, as well as show you an astonishing secret."

The guard hesitated, then enquired, "What secret?"

"Something that will prove that the lady in your crypt was not the queen," I said cautiously, unwilling to play my full hand. I could feel his uncertainty, so pushed on, "If you were to uncover this, you could be hailed a hero, perhaps honoured by the current queen for discovering a traitor."

The guard thought for a while, but soon took the bait. "You're at the wrong gate for a start – meet me over yonder when the light fades."

Henry helped me hop over to where the guard had pointed and we waited with nervous excitement. Unable to believe our luck, we sat in silence wondering if the guard would ever reappear and come through on his promise. Biding my time, I tied some cloth around my ankle for support and tried to put some weight on my injury. It was sore, but at least I was able to limp a short distance with the bandage. Long after the light faded the guard returned and, with help from Henry, I stood up, ready to find my love.

"Just you," he said, pointing at me.

"But I can't walk."

"You can lean on me. I can't risk two of you running loose in the tower." With that he ushered me through the middle tower bridge. I turned to take one final look at Henry, but it was too dark to make out his expression. Once in the inner sanctum I recognised the Tower Green and execution site, and soon we were approaching the chapel. Holding a candle in one hand, the guard opened the main door and led us into the crypt. There, in an open coffin, was the body of a young woman with her head cleanly severed.

"You see," I said victoriously, "her neck is not a bloody mess, it shows that the axe went through just once."

The guard nodded, "Fair enough, you are true to your word. So what's the secret then?"

This time it was my turn to be unsure, because I didn't really want my suspicions to be true. Leaning over the body I took in the face of the girl with whom I had been enamoured and was sure it was Ellie; even in death she was beauteous. I checked the left lobe and sure enough saw the exact childhood scar earned from falling out of a tree. This time there was no doubting what I saw.

"Well, what is it then?" the guard asked, breaking my reverie.

"Take a look at her left ear. I bet you Lady Jane Grey wasn't deformed like that."

The guard peered at Ellie's wound and then back to me. "Is that it? Is that your big secret?" he thundered.

"It may only look like a minor injury, but the implications are enormous."

"How's that, pray tell?"

"It proves that this is not your Queen of Nine Days – someone executed the wrong girl."

"Halt! Who goes there?" came a voice from the back of the crypt. I froze in panic.

"My title is James Morton, Royal Guard to the Palace sir. I thought I saw a vagabond enter the crypt, but I was mistaken, for it is empty." James, as I now knew him to be called, had pushed my head down so that I was crouched, hidden by the table upon which the coffin lay. He artfully engineered the priest out of the crypt and I saw the light of his flame flicker as they walked away from me. Hearing the door shut and a key turn in the lock, I suddenly realised I was trapped, alone in the dark, with the decapitated body of my beloved.

What to do? I could see nothing. I could hear nothing. I could barely move as my aching ankle exposed my foolish naivety. I prayed that James might return to release me when other folk had retired, but as time dragged on I lost hope. I sat on the cold stone floor, propped up against the table and tried to plan my next move. Fatigue caught up with me however and I must have dropped off, for I was rudely awakened by the priest returning early the next morning to set up for mass.

Tentatively trying to stand up I discovered my injury still smarted and my whole body was stiff from an uncomfortable night. Despite the pain, I managed to manoeuvre myself into the shadows at the side of the crypt. With each agonising inch, I edged my way around the outside walls towards the door. I could not just open the door and walk out for fear of attracting unwanted attention to myself, so I had to hope for some suitable scenario in which I could slip away unnoticed. Dawn was breaking and threatened to expose my presence. It was with great relief that the door opened once more to let a stream of clergymen into the crypt.

Seizing the opportunity, I hobbled to the door and scarcely made it through the entrance and back into the shadows before the next group arrived. I was stranded in the courtyard with the shroud of darkness lifting as the morning marched on. My ill-conceived, childish plan to break in to the Tower had somehow succeeded – of a fashion – but I was at a loss as to how I might escape back out of the fortress. Fortune thankfully presented itself once again when traders trundled through the gates pulling the daily supplies on carts. Positioning myself in the shadows near the entrance, I waited until a little queue had formed. Grimacing through the pain in my leg, I territorially placed one hand on a cart and appeared as casual as I could. Limping alongside it, I walked straight out the main gate. The driver on the front bench was oblivious to his role in aiding a stowaway, which was blessed as it was surely a treasonable offence.

With sweat running down my back from both the adrenaline and discomfort, I waited until I was clear of the guards before breaking away from my cover. Outside the tower, I retraced my steps around the walls to the point where James Morton had separated me from Henry. My mucker was curled up in a ball, fast asleep at the foot of a tree. The sound of me hopping over to him made him stir. He jumped to his feet as he recognised my stature, dancing around me.

"I thought you were a goner. Honestly William, I thought they had locked you up in the Tower for good! What happened? Pray where hast thou been?"

Regaling Henry of my adventure, it sounded impossible. I wondered if perhaps it had been a fantasy or a dream. But as I reviewed the story, something about my spiel to James lodged in my brain: if I could prove that the wrong girl was executed, I would be hailed a hero for uncovering treason.

Unsure of how to expose the truth, I knew we urgently required both food and money. Back at the docks we touted for work, but my limp belied my ability to do any manual labour. In a reverse of roles to our first trip to London, merchants were willing to take on Henry, but not me. The man I called brother made me rest by the harbour while he took on every job available to make sufficient money for us both. His generosity warmed my heart, for I had not felt such strong bonds of friendship since I left Rob and Ellie back in Cawston. The memory of which only served to remind me why we were in London; somehow I had to alert the authorities that someone, somewhere had executed the wrong girl.

As Henry slaved away, I daydreamed of being heralded a hero for uncovering some traitor's plot to free Lady Jane Grey and execute an innocent in her place. I fancied I might be rewarded with a handsome sum of money, and perchance be given a title. The North family would surely be eternally grateful that I had deduced what happened to poor Ellie and would keep me in their employ. Perhaps I could even blag a position for Henry, I could honestly vouch for him to be a fine labourer.

***

Henry didn't reappear until the light started to fade and trading ceased for the day. He looked exhausted, but said he was happy to be able to help me out for a change. Thanking him profusely, I motioned to an inn where we both devoured a hot bowl of pottage and bread. Neither of us had any ideas of how to reveal the truth about Ellie and we pondered the problem to no avail.

"Dost thou care for a bit of sport?" asked a hustler.

"What have you on offer?" I asked warily.

"There's a bear out the back ready for a fight."

"Bear-baiting?" I said, my eyes wide open. I had seen cock-fighting plenty of times back in Cawston and Norwich, but had only ever heard rumours of bear-baiting.

"Indeed. If the dog you choose survives, then you double your money."

With my ankle preventing me from working, I felt it was too lucrative an opportunity to turn down. I looked expectantly at Henry and he nodded.

"We're in," I said, hobbling behind the man through the inn to a private courtyard. There, as promised, was a bear – not as big as I had expected – tied to a post. A huge man, his face riddled with scars, paraded a pack of dogs up and down the street. Straining at their leashes I struggled to pick the strongest, but eventually put my money on the ugly white variety with a black eye patch. Henry chose a brindle beast, saying that with two we stood a better chance of winning.

When all bids were placed, scar-face released the hounds and they launched themselves on the bear. A few slashes of those vicious claws put paid to the first couple of dogs, but both of ours were still fighting. The dogs in turn latched their powerful jaws onto the bear's front leg and tried to shake it like a bone. Rearing up onto its hind quarters, the bear swiped one of the beasts away and threw it into a wall, rendering it unconscious. As the bear returned to all fours, three of the canines launched themselves at its neck and started to tear chunks out of its flesh. By the time the proceedings were called to a halt, the bear looked as though it might expire shortly with blood pouring from its neck at an alarming rate. Both our brave hounds remained upright, albeit with multiple gashes down their flanks: we were each awarded double our bets.

Our gamble had paid off handsomely, but now the hustler showed his true colours and proposed a game of dice, no doubt to relieve us of our winnings. Knowing that dice were easily loaded, I declined and we tried to go on our way. Scar-face stopped me and insisted we buy him a beer as a thank you for our prize money; although I felt we were being strong-armed, I was high from the fight and agreed that one celebratory drink couldn't hurt.

I had only ever drunk ale before, but the hustler and scar-face ordered four "double beers", and so that was my first taste of the strong import. After several toasts to our success, the hustler tried to befriend us.

"Pray, tell us travellers, what brings thou hither?"

"We cannot say, for it is forbidden," I replied, keen to end the conversation.

"What can be so sacred as to be forbidden?"

As the alcohol hit my brain, I quickly forgot myself: "A recent secret of a royal nature," I elaborated, miming a slice across my neck with my hand.

This piqued their interest. "Come on my mucker," cajoled scar-face, "we're old friends now, you can tell us your business hither."

Henry tensed beside me. I felt a wave of panic as I realised my loose tongue had led me down a blind alley. It was with a false sense of relief that I recognised the guard, James Morton, and waved boldly to beckon him over to our table. As he strode across the room I stood as if to make introductions, but understood too late that he was in fact at the tavern on official business. Sobering rapidly from my alcoholic haze, I saw he was flanked by two other guards and had cuffs in his hand ready for action.

"We arrest thee in the name of Her Majesty the Queen, on grounds of high treason," said James, placing a heavy iron shackle on one of my wrists. He manhandled me to reach my other arm and clasped the second cuff on it behind my back. Looking around I saw Henry try to protest and being restrained.

As much as I was desperate to argue against the situation, I sensed that this was one of those times when silence was golden and so I motioned to Henry that we should both comply. Parting company from my faithful friend, I was hauled through the streets back to the fated

Tower of London. My mind raced: I frantically tried to work out what had gone wrong. Had I been set up for betting on the bear-baiting? Had the guard told his superior of my attempted break in? Perhaps the priest had discovered my illicit night in the chapel? Had Morton revealed my secret and found it to be false? Whatever the allegation, I deduced I was in serious trouble.

Chapter Ten

Trial without Jury

If you haven't died of shock or blood-loss by then, the beheading will finish you off. Fortunately, you won't know any more than that, but then your body will be divided into four quarters, parboiled to slow decomposition and strung up at Newgate to act as a deterrent to others.

Marching through the pain in my ankle, I was led into the main tower and up a winding stone staircase. After a few flights I was thrown in a cold, bare room.

"Prithy tell me, what is my crime?" I pleaded. The guards remained silent, shutting the door and turning the key in the lock. I had never felt so alone. Panic swept over me in waves, muddling my thoughts as I tried to concentrate on a defence. If only I knew on what grounds I had been arrested.

Hours passed, and then a night in that inhospitable cell. I waited for someone to come, someone to save me, or even just feed me; I remained alone. During daylight I heard noises, voices down the corridor, footsteps on the stairs, but still no one came to my rescue. It was dusk of the second day before I heard the lock turn and the door open a crack. A plate of bread was kicked along the floor, and a bowl of water sloshed where it was dumped at the entrance, before the door was shut and locked once more.

Tearing apart the bread, I devoured the sustenance in a bid to keep up my strength. Dehydration forced me to try the liquid, but it was too rancid to consider consuming. A further night and day passed, with just more bread and dirty water.

Finally, when I thought I might pass out, the door was flung open and two cloaked guards entered the dark room. They led me by the cuffs down several flights of stairs, the rough edges of the shackles cutting my wrists. Although I couldn't see much due to the failing light, the damp, musty air suggested we were going down into a basement. I felt a chill run down my neck as one of my captors illuminated the room with a lamp: it was a torture chamber. Even though I had never seen such instruments before, I couldn't fail to recognise the rack and immediately relieved myself through fear.

"Prithy, don't torture me," I beseeched, "I know nothing. I swear, I haven't done anything." I mentally bargained with God that I would make amends if only He saw it fit to save me from a fate worse than death. But my tormentors continued their preparations, regardless of my protestations. Tears mingled with snot as I collapsed to the floor wailing like a baby. I was petrified at the prospect of what my gaolers had planned.

The men picked me up and pushed me against the rack. Locking my ankles into the heavy restraints, they stretched my arms above my head. My continued caterwauling, asserting my innocence, seemed to fall on deaf ears. With my wrists now attached to the cruel machine, they cranked the winch so that I felt my limbs stretch. There was a pause in the proceedings.

"It is said that you know a royal secret – pray tell us what it is to spare you further pain."

I tried to reply, but words refused to escape my parched mouth.

The winch was cranked again to restore my attention. "Pray tell us what secret you believe to be true or we will continue turning."

Choking on my sobs, I feared I might not be able to save myself as I literally couldn't speak through terror. Naively I had thought I would be branded a hero for exposing a mistaken execution, but now it occurred that perhaps the switch had been deliberate after all and I had in fact revealed a royal cover up. Thinking on my feet I changed my plea.

"I thought," I eventually managed to blurt out, "but I was wrong. I thought I recognised the queen to be someone else, but I was wrong." I repeated my mantra over and over again, stressing my mistake.

Bracing myself for more excruciating pain I was surprised, but mightily relieved, to be freed from the instrument of evil. Spent, I was marched back up to the room and left alone, once more, in the still of the night. Sleep evaded me as I fretted over my predicament. It was of some consolation that I was told Henry had been freed, but I wondered what was to become of me.

***

The sun rose and fell like clockwork as I drifted in and out of consciousness, delirious with cold, hunger and a raging thirst. A few days, or perhaps even a week, passed before the door opened once more. I fantasised about food, freedom, or both. Instead I bore witness to another cloaked silhouette standing in the doorway. I could not see the person's features, but understood that the individual in the entrance would answer my questions.

"It is most unfortunate that you thought you recognised a friend on the block," said the gruff, anonymous voice.

"But I said I was mistaken," I croaked.

"How convenient that your story has changed since you have had time for reflection, but you have been sentenced on your original testimony."

"Sentenced? But I haven't even had a trial."

"You were found guilty of being a traitor and will incur the punishment for an act of high treason: you will be hung, drawn and quartered at Newgate in the morning." The guard turned to leave.

"But I haven't done anything – I beg of you, there must be something that can be done?" I cried, the words catching in my throat as the finality of the situation dawned on me.

My protestations fell on deaf ears however as the heavy door was closed and locked behind the retreating figure. I wanted to weep, but tears refused to roll. I was exhausted. There was nothing left to do other than come to terms with my fate. All I had wanted was to find the truth. Not only had I failed to find out how my beloved Eleanor had been mistakenly executed in the place of Lady Jane Grey, but I had also condemned myself to a horrific end.

My mind played the events of the last few weeks in a constant loop from the moment I heard my ruling. Throughout the long dark hours in the middle of the night I was haunted by images of what might happen the next day. When the first light pierced the chamber, the reality of my future caused dry heaves. I had nothing left to give, yet knew there was much more to come.

The gaoler reappeared at my doorway. He motioned for me to get up, but I was paralysed with fear.

"W-what is going to happen?"

"It's probably best you don't know."

"Please..."

"I am to take you to the main gate where you will be strapped to a sled and tied to the back of a horse. You'll be drawn through the streets to the execution site. There you will be hung up – not dropped like the gallows mind, it won't break your neck. The noose will strangle you, but you'll be cut down before you actually die."

I felt nauseous and light-headed just picturing the scene.

"Then comes the nasty bit: your privy members are cut off and your bowels removed before your eyes and thrown onto a fire. If you haven't died of shock or blood-loss by then, the beheading will finish you off. Fortunately, you won't know any more than that, but then your body will be divided into four quarters, parboiled to slow decomposition and strung up at Newgate to act as a deterrent to others."

My vivid imagination made my stomach heave once more. I spat out the bile I had brought up, then thankfully passed out.

Part III

Chapter Eleven

Hidden Words

...not many people could write Latin, so we were very curious about the author.

Nearly a month after they had bade their farewells, John called Elliot out of the blue. "Do you and the lovely Alice fancy returning to the back of beyond? Tom has come through with the transcription of the manuscript you both found and he says it's very exciting. He won't tell me over the phone – wants a meeting – so I have suggested another dinner at The Horse & Jockey and wondered if you wanted to join us?"

Despite misgivings about the prospects of another evening with Tom, especially one where the expert would be holding all the cards, Elliot was curious as to what secrets the Latin text might hold. "Yeah, that would be great, I know Alice will be tickled pink," he said, mentally racking up the brownie points he would earn. "Why don't we stay at the village B&B this time, save you having to wait on us hand and foot?"

"Don't be daft, old boy, you can stay in the barn, it's no trouble at all," reassured John, completely missing the point that Elliot wanted some creature comforts, not creature companions. Unable to refuse John's insistence, Elliot agreed to drive back to Norfolk that Friday evening to hear what Tom had discovered.

Having been once before the couple found the turning and arrived at John's pile without any delay. Elliot was also mindful to look after his precious car on the long, unsurfaced drive. Once again John came out to greet his guests and fussed around them, taking their bags and bombarding them with questions as to the nature of their journey. Clearly eager to meet up with Tom, John was also conscious to be an attentive host.

"You'll see we've done a bit of work on the old barn," he said modestly. When Elliot rounded the corner, he thought he must have taken a wrong turn as the once-decrepit building was almost unrecognisable. He now understood why John had been so adamant that they stay with him once again: the roof and walls had been repaired, the room cleared, windows cleaned, cobwebs removed, and authentic period furniture stood proud in the cavernous space. The makeshift wash room had been enclosed and turned into a modern, yet sympathetic, en-suite. The guest room was finally fit for guests.

"Oh John, this is amazing," gushed Alice.

"Do you like it?"

"Honestly, this is really beautiful, well done."

"Thanks. I was a little embarrassed after you left that I hadn't suggested you stay at the local B&B, only I hadn't realised quite how bad it was in here. So I put it first on the list of jobs to do. I'm glad you like it. Now I've just to work the same magic on the rest of the house."

"Well, if the end result is anything like this, you'll be onto a winner."

"Yeah, nice job mate," added Elliot, both relieved and impressed.

"So, do you want to freshen up or are you ready to go and meet Tom?" asked John, his face beaming like a kid at Christmas.

"Give me two minutes," replied Alice, "and then I'm all yours."

The old friends chatted about the renovations as they ambled out to the driveway to wait for Alice. She had changed out of her work suit and into jeans and a t-shirt, which was much more fitting for the field walk, and she had tied a cardigan around her waist for the late-night stroll home.

"Ready?" asked John.

"Ready," confirmed Alice. "So, tell us, what has Tom said so far – was I right, was it Latin?"

"Yes, you correctly identified the language–"

"Teacher's pet," ribbed Elliot.

"–but he didn't give much else away. He said that it had taken two experts to translate the script, not because of the language, but because some parts were badly damaged through age. In fact, he said a lot of it was unreadable, but the bits that were legible were very intriguing indeed."

"Nothing more than that? You must be dying to find out."

After a brisk march across the fields to North farm, the trio climbed over the stile leading to the church path. From there, they knew the pub was just a stone's throw away.

John was buzzing with anticipation. He was more than a little disheartened when he turned the wrought iron handle to lift the lever out of the catch to find that Tom was not there waiting for them. Standing at the bar, he ordered drinks and tried to focus on the menu options, but was far too distracted to make any decisions. He jumped at every movement in the pub, each time hoping to see Tom.

Fifteen minutes later the guest of honour stooped as he came through the doorway – a physical reminder of how short the average person was four hundred years ago when the hostelry was built. The tiny entrance was not quite six-foot-high and the ceiling was only a few inches above that, so Tom slouched against the bar while he perused the menu.

"Let's get you a drink, order some food and sit down before you do yourself an injury," suggested Elliot, "unless you want to be plagued by torticollis." He turned to Alice and mouthed the words, "neck ache", to which she thumped him and retorted, "I know what torticollis is, thank you very much; I'm not a complete idiot."

The bar was pretty quiet as most people were enjoying the glow of the late dusk outside, so they were served promptly. Having ordered their meals, John led the way through to the room at the back where he had booked a secluded table. The pitched glass roof refracted the fading light so it acted like a prism, scattering colour across the walls. A waitress delivered a wooden slab piled high with assorted breads and a few accompanying bowls of olives, sundried tomatoes, oil and balsamic vinegar; they were now ready for the big reveal.

"OK guys, here's what we know so far," started Tom, before adding a coverall caveat, "but remember that the documents are yet to be officially verified, so it is still conjecture at this stage."

Alice squealed in delight, "It's like the conclusion of a decent episode of Miss Marple – one with Joan Hickson of course, she's the only believable Miss Marple."

"The only difference being none of us is accused of murder and the suspect has been dead for several hundred years," remarked Elliot.

"Of course, I might kill someone if Tom isn't allowed to tell us what he knows," said John, only half joking.

"Sorry," muttered Alice, pressing her lips together and turning an imaginary lock on her mouth with her fingers.

"The floor's all yours Tom, go ahead," said John.

"Well, there was little doubt that the document could be dated to the mid-to-late sixteenth century. The main part of the manuscript was written as a journal, but there were also a number of loose pages, mostly letters, which had been inserted at various points in the chronology. More perplexing than the contents, was the identity of the author.

"Not many people could write in Tudor times, let alone in Latin. There were a number of references made to 'cousin Mary' and 'cousin Elizabeth', and also mention of the name 'Dudley', however there are precious few other clues as to the journal's owner. Most of the script, in fact the majority of it, was unreadable due to decay, but we could make out that it was originally a month-by-month account of a person's life, which was intermittently completed.

"Essentially, therefore," he concluded, "it affords us a snippet of sixteenth-century living, albeit in a disjointed fashion."

After all the build-up, John looked distinctly deflated.

"I guess just being old isn't sufficient to make something interesting or earth shattering," said Alice trying to lighten the mood. With fortuitous timing the main courses arrived, causing sufficient distraction while everyone digested the news along with their dinner. A stark contrast of tastes and lifestyles was reflected in the food choices: a vibrantly-coloured spectacular-looking salad with minimal calories for Alice; fish and chips for Elliot who preferred to stick to what he knew was good; a piece of venison for Tom who liked the finer things in life; and an enormous steak which was positively still mooing for John. Alice averted her gaze from the almost-raw meat as she wondered how he could eat such a bloody cut without contracting salmonella or botulism.

A preoccupied silence descended as eating commenced, which was only broken by the obligatory questions and comments about the quality of the cuisine. When a slither of each dish had been offered and declined by all parties, Tom picked up where he left off: "Back to the manuscript. You're sort of right Alice: although it's very interesting from a historian's point of view, just being old isn't sufficient enough to make something earth shattering." He paused to chew and swallow a sizeable chunk of what the vegetarian at the table would have called Bambi.

"But, like I said, not many people could write Latin, so we were very curious about the author." Tom took a swig of his drink for dramatic effect. "Between the red wax seal, and the references to 'cousin Mary', 'cousin Elizabeth' and 'Dudley', we deduced that the letters, at least, were penned by Lady Jane Grey."

John gasped. Elliot shook his head looking confused and asked, "I know that name – why do I know that name?"

"The history lesson I gave you last time you were here," exclaimed John, barely able to contain himself once more. "Lady Jane Grey was the Nine Days' Queen. Tom, do you really think the journal is hers?"

"The letters are," he reasserted, "we've crossed-referenced the handwriting and recipients and are sure they are from her. See for yourself." Tom produced a photocopy of some of the writing in Latin and a text book clearly showing a sample of her writing, which looked the same to the untrained eye. Tom then produced translations of some of the text for them all to read.

I write with my truth and grace in the language of God so the account of my life can only be revealed to scholars and the church and the God whom I honour.

O God, according to Thy great mercy, and according to the multitude of Thy tender mercies do away mine offenses. Wash me thoroughly from mine iniquity, and cleanse me from my sin. For I acknowledge my transgressions, my sin is ever before me.

Against Thee only have I sinned, and done this evil in Thy sight: that Thou mayest be justified in thy words, and mayest overcome when Thou art judged. Thou shalt purge me and I shall be clean: Thou shalt wash me, and I shall be whiter than snow. Make me to hear joy and gladness and the bones that have been humbled shall rejoice. Turn away Thy face from my sins: and put out all my iniquities. Create in me a clean heart, O God.

To John Brydges, Lieutenant of the Tower of London, 1554

Live still to die, that by death you may purchase eternal life... As the preacher sayeth, there is a time to be born and a time to die; and the day of death is better than the day of our birth. [3]

To Queen Mary I, 1554

Although my fault be such that but for the goodness and clemency of the Queen, I can have no hope of finding pardon having given ear to those who at the time appeared not only to myself, but also to the great part of this realm to be wise and now have manifested themselves to the contrary, not only to my and their great detriment, but with common disgrace and blame of all, they having with shameful boldness made to blameable and dishonourable an attempt to give to others that which was not theirs and my own lack of prudence for which I deserve heavy punishment it being known that the error imputed to me has not been altogether caused by myself. The Privy Council who with unwanted caresses and pleasantness, did me such reverence as was not at all suitable to my state. He [Dudley] then said that his Majesty had well weighed an Act of Parliament that whoever should acknowledge the most serene Mary or the lady Elizabeth and receive them as the true heirs of the crown of England should be had all for traitors wherefore, in no manner did he wish that they should be heirs of him and of that crown, he being able in every way to disinherit them. And therefore, before his death, he gave order to the Council, that for the honour they owed to him they should obey his last will as to the rest, for my life. [4]

---

[3] Taylor, J.D. (ed) (2004)
[4] Taylor, J.D. (ed) (2004)

John was the first to finish reading the translated passages. “How on earth have these letters ended up in my house, which belonged to a man named George Sawer?”

“Well, that’s what we wanted to know,” continued Tom. “It would appear that he might have been acquainted with Lady Jane Grey, but I’ll come to that later. You’ve obviously heard of our Queen of Nine Days, but do you know her background and how she came to the throne?”

“Funnily enough, I was telling these guys the story last time they were over, but I only know the basics. I know she was forced into marrying Dudley’s son weeks before the young King Edward VI died. And that the king, in turn, was manipulated into changing the line of succession to bypass his half-sisters, Mary and Elizabeth, in favour of their first cousin once removed, Lady Jane Grey. A few days after the sham coronation, Mary assembled her supporters and successfully deposed the usurper. But I’m not too hot on any other details.”

“Well, seeing as I’ve got you here, shall I take you back to the beginning of her story?”

Chapter Twelve

Unhappy Families

Henry VIII knew that Brandon and Mary would be a good match, but, due to sensitive politics of the time with France, the king sent his trusted friend to bring his sister home, on the strict instructions that the two should not yet wed. Brandon broke the promise and married the princess in secret: an act of high treason.

Tom explained that Lady Jane Grey's strict upbringing and the questionable parenting skills of her mother and father had often been highlighted as crucial to her story. He produced a letter which the young teenager had written to her school master, Roger Ascham, in 1550:

My life has been lived through the gracious act of a truly saintly Queen whose words have been honoured as if taken from the Holy Scripture. I find it hard to believe that after this time I have lived I have been so blessed to have followed God's words and reached an end at his will rather than the hand of axeman. My thoughts and life maybe, maybe I will tell you a truth which perchance ye will marvel at. One of the greatest benefits that God ever gave me is that he sent me so sharp and severe parents and so gentle a schoolmaster. For when I am in the presence of Father or Mother, whether I speak, keep silence, sit, stand or go, eat, drink, be merry or sad, be sewing, playing, dancing, or doing anything else, I must do it as it were in such weight, measure and number, even so perfectly as God made the world; or else I am so sharply taunted, so cruelly threatened, yea presently sometimes with pinches, nips and bobs and other ways (which I will not name for the honour I bear them), so without measure misordered, that I think myself in hell, till time comes that I must go to Mr Aylmer, who teacheth me so gently, so pleasantly, with such fair allurements to learning, that I think all the time nothing while I am with him. And when I am called from him, I fall on weeping because whatsoever I do else but learning is full of grief, trouble, fear and wholly misliking to me.[5]

But Tom revealed that things weren't quite as black and white as Jane's letter indicated, for there were many other matters to be taken into consideration to appreciate the whole picture. For a start, the Grey family had an impressive lineage with long-standing royal connections: Henry de Grey received a grant of land from Richard the Lionheart in 1194. One of his descendants, Sir John Grey, married Elizabeth Woodville who, after being widowed and stripped of her dower lands during the War of the Roses, beguiled King Edward IV and became Queen of England. The union produced a number of children – five daughters who survived to adulthood and two sons who famously disappeared, known as the Princes in the Tower. Despite her new royal family, Elizabeth used her position to promote the interests of her two sons by her first

[5] The New Encyclopedia Britannica

marriage and the eldest, Thomas Grey, was created Marquess of Dorset during King Edward IV's reign.

Thomas Grey's son, also called Thomas, was a companion to Charles Brandon, the son of an up-and-coming merchant family who was described as, 'a person comely of stature, high of courage and conformity of disposition to King Henry VIII, with whom he became a great favourite.'[6] Indicative of the king's affection for 'dearest Brandon', Charles took a significant step up the social ladder when he was created Duke of Suffolk.

It wasn't just Henry VIII who was fond of Charles, as the young Princess Mary was smitten with the new duke, despite being betrothed to the King Louis XII. Grey and Brandon had soldiered together into France in 1513, but returned a year later to celebrate the wedding of the king's younger sister, Mary Tudor, and the French king. The marriage was short-lived as the groom, some 30 years the bride's senior, died a few months later.

Henry VIII knew that Brandon and Mary would be a good match, but, due to sensitive politics of the time with France, the king sent his trusted friend to bring his sister home, on the strict instructions that the two should not yet wed. Brandon broke the promise and married the princess in secret: an act of high treason. The Privy Council called for Brandon's head, but due to the king's disposition to his friend and sister, the couple were let off with a heavy fine. They officially married a few months later and went on to have four children, including Lady Frances Brandon.

---

[6] Hanson, M. "Charles Brandon, duke of Suffolk and Princess Mary Tudor" http://englishhistory.net/ tudor/relative/charles-brandon-mary-tudor/, January 31, 2015

When Thomas Grey died in 1530, bidding for the wardship of his son, Henry, was popular amongst the nobility, but was granted to Charles Brandon with the king's approval. This afforded Brandon's eldest daughter, Frances, marriage into the noble Grey family in 1533 and an expedient way to bring two of England's leading families together. Frances was Henry VIII's niece by his younger sister Mary Tudor and Charles Brandon, while Henry Grey was the great-grandson of Elizabeth Woodville, queen of King Edward IV: the marriage was a suitably grand affair, celebrated at Suffolk Place in London.

Mary Tudor died shortly after her daughter's festivities and Charles Brandon remarried, this time to one of his other wards, a thirteen-year-old heiress called Catherine Willoughby who was betrothed to Brandon's youngest son, apparently in order to protect her land. She bore him two sons, and when Brandon died in 1545, they inherited the dukedom of Suffolk. However, the brothers died within an hour of each other from an outbreak of sweating sickness. In 1551, Edward VI fittingly awarded the title, Duke of Suffolk, to Henry Grey, Brandon's son-in-law.

Of five pregnancies, Frances and Henry Grey were blessed with three surviving daughters: Jane born in 1537, Catherine born in 1540, and Mary born in 1545. On King Henry VIII's death, the succession went to his son first, then his female children and then, if they died without issue, to the heirs of Lady Frances. While this technically put the Grey girls in line to the throne, no one anticipated that this bequest would come to fruition. In reality it meant that the family enjoyed a greatly enhanced social status without the restrictions of royalty.

Jane and her two younger sisters were raised at Bradgate in Leicestershire; a grand residence on the edge of Charnwood Forest. When the family were present, visitors could be forgiven for thinking they were already monarchs as celebrations in the Great Hall could accommodate 200 people and meals were served replete with a fanfare. The Greys were rather conceited about their position and heritage, adopting a regal approach whenever they visited the nearby towns and expecting to be treated as leaders of the land.

When they were at Bradgate over the summer months, the Greys spent most of their time hunting and hawking. But both parents preferred to be away from home – Henry took advantage of his position as a prominent peer of the realm by carrying out his social and political duties in London, while his wife chose instead to travel around the country visiting friends, family and other nobility. The children, left back at Bradgate, were well-provided for by proxy via an army of capable servants. Other than a nurse called Mrs Ellen, who would remain with her charge right up until the execution, and the house chaplain, Dr Harding, acting as a tutor in Latin and religious education, little is known about the first decade of Jane's life after her birth sometime in October 1537. It is likely though that she and her sisters would have received a typical education for a girl of nobility: reading and writing, music, dancing and needlework, not to mention good manners and the feminine virtues of obedience and docility.

Jane's parents – her mother in particular – had never shown much affection to her eldest daughter, but, in fairness, the cold relationship was indicative of the time. Jean Luis Vives, the first scholar of the time to study the psyche said that children should not be mollycoddled, 'lest [they] become emboldened to do whatever they like'. He advocated that children should never be indulged – while it was bad for sons, 'it utterly destroyeth daughters'. This was a time when children were expected to be seen and not heard, as well as dutiful and obedient to their parents at all times. If they stepped out of line, strict discipline was administered in order to correct behaviour and build character.

Although this was considered standard practice of the time, and was no doubt treatment to which her sisters were also subjected, Jane resented such practices. She was also a self-righteous madam who openly disapproved of her parents' party-going lifestyle and was disrespectful towards Frances and Henry. She was antagonistic, actively encouraging the chaplain to deliver sermons against gambling, and deriding her parents as 'foolish and irritating' to their friends. If the Greys were unduly harsh on their eldest daughter, perhaps they felt they had just cause?

In 1547, when Lady Jane Grey was entering her pre-teen years and Edward VI had just taken the throne, it was thought by some that the new king might marry his cousin Jane in due course, when they were both ready. They were the same age, of a similar serious nature and, most importantly, fervently Protestant. In the meantime, however, Jane followed the age-old English tradition of being placed out to finish her social education. This practice typically involved a tenure in a household of higher standing and, as the Greys were practically royalty themselves, so it was that the young ingénue emerged onto the social scene by entering Catherine Parr's residence.

Retiring from court after her husband's death and Edward VI's coronation, the dowager queen remained close to London in her comfortable red brick building in Chelsea, overlooking the Thames in the suburbs of the capital. Catherine Parr had been the most likeable of Henry's wives and was known for her warm, kind, open nature. Keen to be a good stepmother, she was already friends with Mary, having likely grown up together, and made a particularly good impression on the youngest two, Elizabeth and Edward. While Edward took the throne, Elizabeth joined Catherine at the dower house. Although Elizabeth and Jane lived together and would have been in regular contact – at lessons, mealtimes, prayers and social events – there is no indication that the two girls were close. Jane was still considered a child at nine years old, while Elizabeth was, according to reports, a proud and disdainful thirteen-year-old who might have been domineering company for a shy girl like Jane.

Catherine was well-educated and thoughtful, and created a learning environment under her roof which became known as the centre of the Protestant 'New Learning'. That the household was so inviting, as well as being the scene of frequent religious instruction and debates, offered Lady Jane, for the first time in her young life, true happiness and a sense of belonging. She was a quiet and studious girl by nature and positively thrived in the nurturing environment, becoming increasingly devout to her religion through the teachings of Catherine's household. Although she had been raised Protestant, she dismissed her parents' choice of religion as a result of political necessity and believed that she was a better servant to her faith because she truly understood its tenets.

Before Henry VIII laid claim to her, Catherine had been set to marry the love of her life, Thomas Seymour and, on the king's death, she was now free to be with him. As Edward VI's uncles, the Seymour brothers were powerfully influential during the reign of the young king. The elder, Edward Seymour, was the Lord Protector, while the younger, Thomas, was resentful of his sibling's authority and disappointed he only possessed a baronetcy, seat on the Privy Council and a new office of Lord Admiral. A secret marriage to the dowager queen, probably in April 1547, followed by a move into her house with two young girls in line to the throne, helped Thomas redress the balance.

Despite being the King of England, Edward VI was kept remarkably short of money by Uncle Edward, his Lord Protector, so Thomas tried to curry favour with generous clandestine gifts of pocket money. An intelligent and sensitive soul, Edward felt both indignant to the hardship borne by Edward and manipulated by the furtive bribes from Thomas. Still, supporters of Edward Seymour were openly rewarded for their loyalty and John Dudley became Earl of Warwick.

Desperate to beat his brother in the royal power struggle, Thomas tried another tactic to secure future influence on the royal household – he used his charm on Princess Elizabeth with increasingly indiscreet behaviour. Becoming overly familiar with the young girl, he would burst into her bedroom in his nightgown to wake her up, tickle her in bed, smack her bottom playfully and engage in raucous games of hide-and-seek. Thomas was warned to desist such inappropriate antics by Elizabeth's governess, but the matter was raised to Catherine when he refused to comply. The dowager queen diffused the situation temporarily and overlooked the misdemeanour as she loved Thomas passionately.

Hedging his bets, Thomas turned his attentions to the other young heiress in his midst, but he did not try and engage Lady Jane in such intimate romps; it is possible that she was not physically mature enough for him, but also likely that she would not have entertained such disgraceful behaviour. Instead, Thomas befriended the Greys and sent his trusted servant, John Harington, to talk to Jane's father, Henry Grey. The two accounts vary: Harrington claimed he was instructed to open negotiations to suggest that awarding Jane's wardship to Thomas would likely lead to her marriage to the king; Grey however recalled an explicit guarantee of a royal pairing and entered into a covenant to sell his daughter's custody to Thomas for the handsome sum of £2,000, with a down payment being made of a few hundred pounds and the remainder promised in instalments.

Relations between the two Seymour brothers deteriorated. Edward disapproved of Thomas' marriage to Catherine and tried to claim royal ownership some of Catherine's jewellery. His wife, too, was hostile to Catherine, infuriated that the dowager queen was more entitled than the Lord Protector's wife at state events. When Thomas was actually caught by Catherine in a compromising embrace with her step-daughter, Elizabeth, it was Catherine's actions alone that averted a national scandal and disgrace as she sent the princess to visit some family friends in Cheshunt. This swift and gracious reaction not only saved Catherine much embarrassment, but preserved her husband's reputation.

Jane remained with Catherine and Thomas after the incident and accompanied them to Sudeley Castle, their pile in Gloucestershire, in June 1548 when Catherine was heavily pregnant. On 30 August, Catherine gave birth to a baby daughter, Mary, but within a week the new mother had died of puerperal fever – a common complication after childbirth and something from which Jane Seymour had also passed away. Jane was evidently very fond of

Catherine and must have been devastated by the development. One can only imagine the sorrowful sight of the girl, who was petite for her age, freckled and with red hair, acting as chief mourner when Catherine was buried in the chapel at Sudeley.

Frances and Henry Grey had been disappointed that no match had been made with their daughter and the king in the year since her wardship had been purchased, and so used Catherine's death as an excuse to take back control. They wrote to Thomas Seymour, offering their condolences and requesting that Jane be returned home when Catherine's household was dispersed. They explained that she was too young to left without guidance and should resume the governance of her mother, "lest she should, for lack of a bridle, take too much head" and unlearn all the good behaviour bestowed upon her by the dowager queen. What they failed to mention was that they were thinking of offering Jane in marriage to the Lord Protector's son instead.

Having gone too far with Elizabeth, Thomas could not let his grasp on Jane slip out of his hands. His compromise was to let Jane return home during September 1548 while he negotiated hard with the Greys to retain his claim on her. From the bosom of a loving and lively family, Jane found herself once again back in a home devoid of affection. Greeted by the return of physical abuse such as pinching and smacking, Jane objected to her parents' methods of discipline as much as she disapproved of their continued wickedness of gambling, socialising and devotion to material gain. She wrote to Thomas Seymour from Bradgate to assure him that she would obey him like a father if she were permitted to return.

Keen to relieve themselves of any duty for their arrogant daughter, the Greys were delighted to hire a tutor to continue Jane's education. She retained her conscientious study under the guidance of John Aylmer, a friend of Roger Ascham who was a former tutor of Princess Elizabeth whom Jane had once met. Indeed, that encounter impressed Ascham so greatly that he preserved it in his educational treatise, The Schoolmaster. After a month or so, Thomas renewed his promise to see that the king married Jane and secured Jane's wardship once more from the greedy, power-hungry Greys with another down-payment of £500.

Jane was grateful to be away from her parents, but the Seymour household was not the same without Catherine. Thomas' battle for power had lost gravitas with the death of his wife, the dowager queen, and he began openly canvassing support from peers. It seemed that he was oblivious to the lack of backing he received regarding his plans to diminish the power of the Lord Protector. Keen to re-establish his position, Thomas renewed his interest in Princess Elizabeth, delving into her financial affairs and encouraging rumours that he would take her as his next wife. The dangerous game Thomas was playing not only displeased his brother and members of the Privy Council, but made King Edward VI suspicious that he would be overthrown by his uncle.

While John Dudley, the new Earl of Warwick, had publicly supported Edward, in fact he had intended to destroy both the Seymour brothers so that he could take the title and influence of Lord Protector for himself. Dudley astutely gauged Thomas' arrogance and ambition to be a tool with which he could bring them both down.

On 17 January 1549, Thomas Seymour was arrested at Seymour Place in London on numerous charges of treason for disloyal practices, predominantly relating to the young princess. Interrogations on Elizabeth's household revealed the inappropriate behaviour, but the astute teenager did well not to incriminate Thomas for any conspiracy. The Greys, who had immediately reclaimed Jane amidst the controversy, were also investigated and Henry admitted he had been foolishly 'seduced and aveugléd' into co-operating with Thomas' plans for his daughter. In a bid to save his own reputation with the Privy Council, Henry Grey even offered Jane's hand in marriage to the Lord Protector's eldest son, but nothing came of the proposal.

Rather than disturbing Parliament, which was in session, a bill of attainder was prepared and passed through both Houses by early March. The guilty verdict without the need for a trial required one last signature – that of the Lord Protector, Thomas's elder brother. Edward Seymour deliberated for a week, presumably wrestling with his conscience, which afforded Dudley the opportunity to take control. Dudley urged the Privy Council to appeal to the king to make the decision without troubling the Lord Protector further. King Edward VI cared little for either of his Seymour uncles and so duly signed the bill. Thomas Seymour was executed on Tower Hill on 20 March, 1549.

But Dudley hadn't finished: the megalomaniac moved to take control of the government.

The year of 1549 was one of social discontent, marked by rising prices, high unemployment and a bad harvest. Added to this, people resented the radical religious changes that were coming into force. There were two acute revolts which distressed the land-owning gentry; one in the West Country and one in Norfolk. Responsibility for all of these disastrous events lay at the Lord Protector's door. Furthermore, Edward Seymour had lost public support since he had been seen to allow the execution of his own brother – a reaction Dudley had accurately anticipated. Conversely, Dudley was a capable soldier who had quashed the West Country rebellion, pleasing both landowners and the king. This gave him the backing of the gentry and the support of a well-armed and experienced group of soldiers surrounding him.

By the beginning of October, Edward Seymour knew his rule was in jeopardy and he took the king to the fortified Windsor Castle, under the weak guise of seeking safety. His young charge sensed the abduction and wrote, "Me thinks I am in prison". Seymour was arrested and taken to the Tower, while Dudley emerged as leader of the council, although he sagely refused the title of Lord Protector. Instead he regained his title of Lord High Admiral – a post reluctantly relinquished to Thomas Seymour. Dudley's coup coincided with the king's physical maturation and interest in sport, so he was able to manipulate Edward VI, not by paternalistic control, but through flattery and empowerment of money and physical freedom.

By October 1551, Dudley had been sufficiently emboldened through his relationship with the king to petition him for a new title and he was made Duke of Northumberland as a reward for two years of Edward's favour. As such, was the first man who had no ties of marriage or blood to the reigning royal family to receive a ducal title.

Chapter Thirteen

For Better, or for Worse?

An upper-class Tudor girl refusing to enter a matched marriage could anticipate a beating until she changed her mind. For Lady Jane Grey, we can only imagine the wrath that might have been borne on her if she had refused any of the arrangements.

Tom had been so engrossed in detailing Lady Jane Grey's background, he was dismayed to note when he had finished that most of his dinner remained on the plate, cold and untouched. His companions, on the other hand, had polished off their food and were leaning back on their seats, enraptured by the complex tale of incestuous relationships and political subterfuge.

"OK," said John, "we get that Lady Jane Grey was an innocent pawn in the whole sorry mess. She had been offered in marriage to a number of people in return for political power, and had been passed around from pillar to post – but it sounds like she was a smart cookie, so how did she finally get pushed into a marriage with Dudley's son?"

"To understand that, I think you need to remember what was considered the norm for the period. There were no suffragettes, women's lib didn't exist and no one spoke of equal rights. Jane might have been well educated, but she was still expected to fulfil the role of a woman, which was generally to get married and bear as many children as possible. Because a lot of infants died before they were toddlers, and plenty more didn't make it beyond teenage years, it was common for women to have multiple births, sometimes up to nine or ten.

"Given the short life expectancy of the time, a juvenile woman would be married off, perhaps as an early teenager, to an older, wealthy gentleman who still required a male heir, or a spare. The girl would then inherit her husband's land and money on his death and be free to marry again. An upper-class Tudor girl refusing to enter a matched marriage could anticipate a beating until she changed her mind. For Lady Jane Grey, we can only imagine the wrath that might have been borne on her if she had refused any of the arrangements.

"Don't forget that the European reformers were hopeful that King Edward VI would marry his virtuous cousin to make England the most blessed Protestant realm. It was typical of the royal household that the two English princesses were not present when Mary of Guise, mother of Mary Queen of Scots and Regent of Scotland, visited England in November 1551. Instead, Frances and Henry Grey were there to present their fourteen-year-old daughter and the occasion at Hampton Court marked Jane's official debut on the English political scene.

"The following year, when Jane contracted an illness her parents reprimanded her for devoting too much time to study and not enough to social concerns. While they realised an educated daughter was an asset, it was far more profitable to have one who could attract a wealthy, influential spouse."

"Other than offering their daughter's hand in marriage to whoever suited them most at the time, were Jane's parents really monsters?" Alice asked incredulously. "I thought you said that what they did was normal for the era and that she was not exactly an easy child."

"Well, the accusations of abuse are built on a story related over a decade after Jane was beheaded. Roger Ascham published a book called The Schoolmaster in 1570 – you will remember that he was friends with Jane's tutor, John Aylmer, and the two conversed regularly about his student. In his text, the young Jane Grey is described as reading Plato's Phaedo in Greek while the rest of the household was out hunting. He relates Jane's own admission in the letter I showed you earlier that she loved learning, because lessons with her kindly tutor were a respite from the abuse of her parents if she didn't perform every task perfectly. 'I am so sharply taunted, so cruelly threatened, yea presently sometimes with pinches, nips and bobs and other ways (which I will not name for the honour I bear them),' Ascham recalled her saying.

"However, there are always two sides to the coin. Jane also had the privilege of knowing John ab Ulmer, a Swiss theologian and student of Henry Bullinger, chief pastor of the Protestant church in Zurich. Both Ulmer and Bullinger were friends of Aylmer and Ascham, and the four men discussed Jane's education at some length. Jane's spiritual and intellectual horizons were expanding as she read the Gospels and other religious works, alongside all the Greek classics. As well as Latin, she could read, write and speak Greek and embarked on Hebrew, being hailed as a prize student by the esteemed quartet teaching her.

"Many of the letters have survived which show that while Lady Jane Grey was obviously a diligent student, she was also growing into an independent, head-strong young woman. In one letter, Aylmer was concerned that Jane was too interested in her appearance, with trivial matters such as dresses, jewels and hair braidings, as well as spending too much time on her music. Furthermore, Aylmer's letters also reveal her challenging manner, of which her parents had tired: he complained that Jane, 'was at that age [when]... all people are inclined to follow their own ways,' and he asked how best to, 'provide bridles for restive horses,' meaning that she was a spirited girl."

"So how did Dudley persuade this spirited girl to marry his son?" asked Elliot.

Before Tom began the next part of the tale, he suggested everyone refreshed their drinks and took a comfort break. When they were all settled once more, he continued to explain the plan Dudley masterminded.

***

Since replacing Edward Seymour as the king's closest advisor, John Dudley had shown his naked ambition as he became the true power behind the throne. The Princesses, Mary and Elizabeth, had rarely attended the king's court, and Dudley realised that if either half-sister were to take the crown, he would most certainly lose his influential position and, in the case of Mary's ascension, possibly even his head. This concern plagued all the Protestant lords who had prospered during King Edward VI's six-year reign, not just Dudley. He had talked of retiring from political life, but that was only a passing dream as he had made too many enemies – particularly the Catholic nobility and churchmen – for that to be viable.

Dudley saw few opportunities available to him to retain his position of influence. Mary, a staunch Catholic, had tried to pretend that Edward was a misguided Protestant puppet, but couldn't accept it when he, like Henry before him, had ordered her to change her religion as her king. Dudley realised he would have no sway over her. One possibility he considered in passing was a marriage between Princess Elizabeth and his only bachelor son, Guildford Dudley. The truth, however, was that Elizabeth Tudor, at nearly twenty years old, possessed seasoned political acumen and would never acquiesce to being Dudley's patsy.

The only route, he deduced, was via Jane Grey, fourth in line for succession after her mother Frances. Dudley gauged that she would be amenable enough and so, picking up where Thomas Seymour had left off, Dudley began plotting with Jane's equally ruthless parents to solve his little problem. His first step was to take over as Jane's ward, then he had to convince the Greys that their daughter, the first eligible female in the line of succession to the throne, should marry his last unmarried son, Lord Guildford Dudley. Finally, he would have to get Frances to agree to forego her own superior claim to the crown in favour of her daughter.

In the spring of 1552, the fifteen-year-old king fell ill with measles. Although he recovered well enough to attend the St George's Day services at Westminster Abbey and maintain his sporting activities – notably jousting, playing tennis and going hunting – it left him weakened. Over the summer of that year, Edward VI began his most extensive tour through the south and west of the country. Thanks to Dudley's handling, the adolescent king enjoyed having the opportunity to travel so far out of the capital, however after the earlier illness he found the pace exhausting. Passers-by could have been forgiven for thinking he was seriously ill: he was pale, had lost his appetite and, subsequently, substantial weight.

When the king returned to Windsor in mid-September he was further troubled by tuberculosis; by Christmas 1552, his condition was so obvious that the holiday celebrations were disproportionately extravagant to draw attention away from Edward's failing health. In his condition his heir, Princess Mary, commanded greater respect, yet when she came to visit in February 1553, his illness prevented their meeting for three days. On 11 April 1553, Edward moved his household to Greenwich Palace as he thought he would be more comfortable in his favourite residence. Although the king had managed to open parliament in March, he was clearly suffering with considerable pain, holding one shoulder higher than the other, and looking very drawn.

With Edward apparently dying, there was no possibility of him marrying Jane and so, swayed by the possibility of wealth and power, the Greys hungrily agreed to Dudley's plan for Jane to marry Guildford. Jane predictably protested the union, but was persuaded by, "the urgency of her mother and the violence of her father"; in other words, by verbal and physical abuse.

It is unlikely that Jane objected on the grounds that she didn't like Guildford. Like most of the Dudley men he was handsome enough, he was fair-haired and about her age. Admittedly he might have been arrogant and spoilt by his mother, but he had no other documented flaws and, compared to other eligible suitors, he was an acceptable match. Her concern was much more likely to have been aimed almost entirely at his father. Like most of the population, Jane disliked and distrusted John Dudley. The duke's plan to manoeuvre Jane into position was to play on her most passionate cause. He knew that the staunch Protestant didn't want to see Catholic Mary as queen any more than he did. Jane's tutor, Aylmer, had recorded that even before the crises of 1553 that Jane had snubbed gifts from Mary Tudor, whom she condemned as, "against God's Word". Jane's opposition to Edward's heir was based on religious principles, while Dudley's was pure Machiavellianism.

To this end, Jane was bullied into marrying a young man she hardly knew and becoming the daughter-in-law of a man she hated. The couple's betrothal was announced in the spring and, after a brief courtship, the celebration took place on 25 May 1553. The event was held at the Dudley's London residence, Durham House, which was one of the great homes of Tudor England. It was, in fact, a triple wedding – along with the union of Jane and Guildford, Jane's younger sister, Catherine, married Lord Herbert, while Guildford's younger sister, Katherine, wed Lord Hastings. Orders, signed by the king, had been sent to the Master of the Wardrobe so that the grandest clothing and jewels could be used. Edward VI himself was supposed to attend, but was far too poorly by then to be able to watch his cousin march down the aisle, richly apparelled in a gown of gold and silver brocade, her red hair braided with pearls.

It would appear that Jane and Guildford's marriage marks the beginning of Dudley's scheming to change the line of succession, but the truth is that King Edward VI had confided his concerns about his Catholic heir ever since he realised he was dying. Just as Mary believed Catholicism was the path to righteousness, Edward was committed to Protestantism. He felt that as king, charged by God, he was responsible for his subjects' religious welfare and wanted his nation – for its own sake, for his immortal soul and for the royal legacy – to remain Protestant. He told his trusted advisor that Mary had to be prevented from leading England on the path to damnation.

So, from the end of 1552 to the beginning of 1553, Edward created his Device for the Succession. Initially he left the throne to Lady Frances Grey and her male heirs, followed by Lady Jane Grey and her male heirs, but it was apparent that Frances would have no more children and none of her daughters would bear children in time. So he made another change which lit the fuse for an almighty explosion: he simply named his succession to the throne as 'the Lady Jane and her heirs male'. It was the beginning of the end for Lady Jane Grey.

Edward's Device for the Succession was eventually issued with the title, Letters Patent for the Limitation of the Crown, and in it he clearly disinherited the Princesses, Mary and Elizabeth, because they were "illegitimate and not lawfully begotten". Being only half-sisters of the king, he argued that they were not entitled to succeed him and, echoing his father's concerns, he reasoned that they might marry foreign husbands who would 'tend to the utter subversion of the commonwealth of this our realm'. However, despite being published, Edward's device remained invalid as long as Henry VIII's 1544 Act of Succession was acknowledged by parliament. Without enough time to have the act superseded, Dudley advised his king that they only needed to gain support from government to complete the plan.

To this end, Dudley spent June 1553 advocating the Privy Council, as well as leading members of the judiciary and church, to endorse the new device. He started with political persuasion, but was not averse to more bullying tactics where required. The Lord Chief Justice, Sir Edward Montague, and the Archbishop of Canterbury, Thomas Cranmer, were uneasy with the alteration, but Dudley labelled them traitors and advised the king to order their obedience. After that, Edward's device was recognised by the Lord Chancellor, the Privy Councillors, twenty-two peers of the realm, the Lord Mayor of London, various aldermen and sheriffs, the secretaries of state and key judges and churchmen. The Letters Patent for the Limitation of the Crown was endorsed with the Great Seal on 21 June, not a moment too soon: King Edward VI died in the early evening of Thursday, 6 July, 1553.

***

While Dudley had been busy pushing through the change of succession, Lady Jane Grey had suffered the ignominy of being married to Guildford Dudley for almost six weeks. Disliking her in-laws even more than her parents, Jane insisted she depart the Dudley household after the wedding in favour of Suffolk Place in Westminster, before moving into her parents' new residence in London, a former Carthusian monastery. Jane's new mother-in-law did not approve of this arrangement and was just as persuasive as the dastardly duke. She immediately informed the Greys that as the king was dying, Jane, the heir to his throne, must be ready and waiting to act as required. In no uncertain terms, Jane was to return to the Dudley house.

Jane later claimed that this was the first she knew of Edward's impending death, but at the time she acted out, every bit the teenager that she was. She rebuked the duchess' claim as being overly dramatic and a means for the Dudleys to steal her from her parents. In return the duchess reproached the Greys for keeping the newlyweds apart. In the end, there was no real reason Jane should not be with her husband and so she returned to Durham House, and possibly consummated her marriage.

After a few days with her in-laws, Jane became ill and claimed she was being poisoned. The accusation, like her previous outburst, was ludicrous and exposed her naivety in the world of politics – why would the Dudleys ruin their chance of power by harming their greatest asset? Understandably concerned with Jane's physical and mental state, the duchess sent her to Catherine Parr's former home in Chelsea where Jane had once been so happy, to help her relax.

It was there, on Sunday, 9 July, that Dudley's eldest daughter, Mary Sidney, visited Jane. She said, in all seriousness, that they were to leave Chelsea for Syon House, a former convent on the Thames which Dudley controlled.

Chapter Fourteen

Jana Regina

She [Jane] was greeted with unaccustomed affection and reverence, with many kneeling before her and kissing her hand. Jane blushed, both embarrassed and bemused by their references to her as their sovereign lady.

As Tom detailed how Lady Jane Grey had been married off in a hurry and was poised to take the throne, the other three around the table had been gripped and the empty glasses in front of them went unnoticed. Having answered the direct question he had been asked, the story teller paused and simply said, "I'm parched."

"Of course, let me get you another," said John. "Same again, everyone? Does anyone care for any pudding?"

Alice and Elliot both raised a glass to accept another drink, but groaned and held their stomachs in appreciation of their dinner to decline the offer of dessert. Tom, on the other hand, had not eaten all of his main as he had been so busy talking that he asked John to get him something gooey and chocolatey.

When John came back from the bar, he and Alice went to ask the next question at the same time.

"One at a time," laughed Tom.

"Ladies first," offered John graciously.

"I just wanted to know what happened next – what was your question, John?"

"I still want to know how come Lady Jane Grey's papers ended up with George Sawer in what is now my house?"

"Fair enough, you win I guess," she conceded.

"Actually, I kind of need to answer Alice first and finish the tale," explained Tom. "But I will get to your very good question before closing time, John, I promise." And so he picked up where he left off: that Jane and Guildford had married and Jane was being transported to Syon House on matters of grave importance.

While Jane had claimed not to have known that Edward was dying – despite his ghostly appearance – it is not clear whether or not she was aware of the extent of Dudley's duplicity. Of course she appreciated her own lineage, that she was fourth in line for the English throne, after the princesses, Mary and Elizabeth, and her own mother, Frances Grey. She must have wondered why both John Dudley and her parents were so anxious for her to marry Guildford as quickly as possible. And she surely would have questioned the fact that her sister wed into another influential noble family on the same day. She undoubtedly suspected some, if not all, of Dudley's plan, but in the event, any awareness of the plot was probably a greater strain than blissful ignorance.

Of course, even if she knew Dudley intended to by-pass the princesses and make her his puppet queen, there was precious little she could have done to prevent him. She could do nothing to escape her family or in-laws and she was, quite literally, trapped. The charge of poisoning was probably a cry for help as a result of nervousness and hysteria.

On her arrival at Syon House, Jane found a welcoming committee made up of her parents, in-laws, and a variety of distinguished nobles including the earls of Arundel, Huntington and Pembroke, as well as the Marquess of Northampton. She was greeted with unaccustomed affection and reverence, with many kneeling before her and kissing her hand. Jane blushed, both embarrassed and bemused by their references to her as their sovereign lady.

Dudley then led her into the Chamber of State in a formal procession and guided her onto a dais reserved for royalty. Dudley, in his capacity as President of the Council, gave a lengthy speech in which he announced the death of King Edward VI. He proclaimed that the young king had led a "virtuous life" and had always cared for his kingdom, which is why he had decided that his sisters were disinherited having been deemed unworthy, and that he would appoint his cousin, Jane, as his successor to the throne.

Perplexed that such a cataclysmic event as Edward's death could have been hidden from her or the general public, Jane stood rooted to the spot, trembling. She may have suspected the reason for the pomp, but the actual moment of declaration was too much for her. She later wrote that the knowledge had left her, "stupefied and troubled". She was speechless. As the gathered crowd all knelt before her again, she collapsed to the floor in tears. No one moved to console or help her up, but through her sobs she was heard to mutter that she was "insufficient for the task," and he was, "such a noble prince." When she regained enough control, Jane said, "The crown is not my right and pleaseth me not. The Lady Mary is the rightful heir." Regardless of how the situation had arisen, it is likely that she didn't care for such a responsibility and instead wished for solitude and to return to her studies.

The ingratitude of the queen-to-be was admonished first by Dudley and then by her own parents, no doubt thinking of their own position. The Greys demanded that she did as she was told and undertake the duties required of her. The puritan Jane felt she must obey her parents and so, reluctantly, agreed, all the while insisting she was inadequate to fulfil the role. Dismissing her self-deprecation as a teenager being overwhelmed, the Lords of the Council took a solemn oath to shed their blood in defence of her claim. Jane murmured a quick prayer that if it was God's will that she be queen, then she would trust in God to help her govern England for His glory.

Her reaction was the opposite of what had been expected by the select nobility present at the momentous occasion – she was not remotely excited, or even pleased at the prospect and worse still, she was far from gracious. They could have been forgiven for wondering why they had been intimidated into pronouncing Queen Jane. Regardless, the fact remained that she was pronounced as the heir to the throne and – for nine long days – Queen Jane ruled England.

***

John Dudley had clearly spent a great deal of time plotting exactly how he would manoeuvre the unwilling Jane into the position of queen so that his son, in turn, would be king. But that in itself was not enough: he needed to negate the opposition posed by the usurped princesses. He believed that a quick coup, eliminating any potential threats, was the key to success.

On hearing the inevitable news of King Edward's death, Dudley persuaded the Council to send a letter to the princesses, each in their respective Hertfordshire palaces; Mary at Hunsdon and Elizabeth at Hatfield. In the correspondence, Dudley omitted the truth, telling them only that Edward was very ill and wished to see his half-sisters. The duke also managed to control sources to keep the real news out of the public domain. Mary, who had been anxious to hear news of her brother, fell for the deception and immediately started a trip to London to see her younger sibling on his deathbed. Dudley meanwhile set up a trap to have Mary seized en route and taken to the Tower as a prisoner.

Mary, the daughter of Catherine of Aragon, was much-loved by the English population as they had always been sympathetic to her mother's plight. The general public rejected the claim that Mary's was illegitimate, as Catherine had only been forced aside by the king's lust for Anne Boleyn and desire for a male heir. When Mary reached Hoddesdon, a reliable sympathizer informed her of the king's actual demise and warned her of Dudley's plot. Mary turned back and took half a dozen attendants, first to Cambridge, then on to Kenninghall in Norfolk. Not only was Mary popular in East Anglia, but the less wealthy locals also hated Dudley for quashing the Kett's Rebellion. Furthermore, the proximity to the coast meant that she could flee and seek refuge within the Spanish Netherlands, if necessary.

It was not long before Mary received further confirmation of her brother's death and so, with the news gathering a pace, she sent a carefully-worded letter to the Council, in which she asked them to recognise her as Queen, assuming that she was the rightful heir to the throne. She excluded any knowledge of Dudley's plot, but expressed her surprise that, as heir to the throne, she hadn't been informed of her brother's death until two days after the event. The letter arrived on 9 July, by which time Jane had already been pronounced queen at Syon House.

Most historians agree that Dudley had subjugated and terrorised the Council into following his will in the face of this counterclaim. He upheld the three reasons that Mary was not fit for the throne; her mother's divorce from Henry VIII, her Catholicism and her gender. The Council agreed under duress to move forward with their plan to declare Jane as queen, and tell Mary it was already done when she eventually arrived. In the meantime, they responded to the princess' letter in a matter-of-fact manner: to reinforce her illegitimacy and inability to inherit 'the Crown Imperial of this realm', and encourage her to demonstrate her obedience to the Sovereign Lady Queen Jane by turning herself over to the authorities. It was not the response for which Mary had hoped.

Dudley might have thought he had succeeded, but he also understood the power of the general consensus and recognised the limits of his support – the vast majority of the nobility were unlikely to rally for an unpopular bully in the face of valid opposition. When he realised that Mary had fled rather than journeyed into his ambush, he had been forced to proceed with the coup on 9 July without having first secured the main contender. To promote his cause, he had the Bishop of London preach against the princesses at St Paul's Cross, shaming them as bastards and singling out Mary as a papist who was bent on destroying the country's religion. To conclude matters, Dudley sent his s son Robert to capture Princess Mary.

Elizabeth, meanwhile, remained in the country. She was no admirer of her half-sister Mary, but knew that if Jane Grey was recognised as queen, her own claim to the crown would be automatically forfeited. So she chose the safest course of action: inaction. Elizabeth feigned a convenient illness and remained quiet, neither supporting nor rejecting Jane, like all of England and most of Europe, just watching and waiting.

On Monday, 10 July 1553, Queen Jane was taken in full state from Syon House to Westminster. Dressed in the green and white of the Tudors for her first public appearance, she wore raised wooden shoes called chopines to make her seem grander and giving her an extra three inches of height. Guilford, her husband was garbed with equal splendour, adorned in white and gold. They travelled via a parade of barges to the Dudley residence, Durham House, where they dined, before journeying, again by barge, to the Tower of London.

It was an ancient custom that each new sovereign must go to the Tower to assume its possession at the beginning of his or her reign. So, between three and four o'clock Jane and her attendants arrived at the Tower where the crown jewels had been laid out and the state apartments were prepared to receive the new queen. Rather than a rapturous applause along the route, the crowds on the river banks were mostly silent and quizzical. King Edward VI's death had not long since been announced and during their mourning they were confronted with a young, unwanted and unknown cousin claiming the throne with great pomp. The public felt that Mary was the rightful heir and did not support this perceived interloper.

The Marquess of Winchester and Sir John Bridges, the Lieutenant of the Tower, greeted Lady Jane. Winchester knelt to present the keys of the fortress, but it was Dudley, not Jane, who stepped forward to collect them, indicating exactly who would be the driving force behind the throne. A gun salute was heard around 5:00pm, while the late afternoon sun highlighted the silken flags and gilded decorations.

There was an eyewitness account by a Genoese merchant named Baptista Spinola, who was standing with a group of spectators outside the main Tower gates waiting to catch a glimpse of this new queen. He wrote of Lady Jane Grey:

'She is very short and thin, but prettily shaped and graceful. She has small features and a well-made nose, the mouth flexible and the lips red. The eyebrows are arched and darker than her hair, which is nearly red. Her eyes are sparkling and reddish brown in colour. Her complexion was good, unmarked by the pox, but freckled; she had sharp white teeth and a lovely smile. Because she was so short, she wore chopines; these were shoes with a special cork sole designed to make her appear taller. Her gown was made of green velvet stamped with gold (the colours undoubtedly flattered her red hair).'[7]

Spinola wrote of her husband, Guildford:

'[He is] a very tall strong boy with light hair and clothed in white and silver velvet. [He] paid her much attention.'[8]

Lady Jane proceeded into the White Tower where she was installed in the royal apartments. Away from the pomp and ceremony, and behind closed doors, another rift occurred between Jane and the Dudleys, far more serious

---

[7] Davey, R. (2008) p82

[8] Davey, R. (2008) p82-3

than the first. The Lord Treasurer, the Marquess of Winchester, brought a selection of the royal jewels for the new queen to try on, among which was the crown. Jane would later stress that she had never asked for the crown, and that it was brought to her without request. Winchester wanted to check if it fitted properly, but Jane refused to try it on. She had complied with Dudley's desire for her to be queen for nearly twenty-four hours, but wearing the most sacred symbol of the monarchy was a step too far. In her mind, if she put it on it would be as though she condoned the deed. Winchester didn't understand the reason for her hesitation, and so to put her at ease he reassured her that another would be made to crown her husband king.

As Jane finally realised the extent of the plan, she saw that Dudley didn't care whether or not England was a righteous nation, nor about Edward's will, he wanted to maintain control of the country and to turn his family into royalty.

Jane, a Tudor herself and proud of her royal blood, was outraged. The Dudleys, an arrogant, pretentious family, had no right to exploit her. Laying down the gauntlet for her reign she told those assembled that she would gladly make Guildford a duke, but he would never be king. Guildford, typically, rushed to fetch his mother and the pair launched a verbal attack on the new queen, trying to terrorise her into acquiescing and crowning him king. When Jane stood her ground, Guildford and his mother announced they would be leaving for Syon House.

Ironically, having been desperate to separate herself from her husband at the start of their marriage, there was no way Jane could allow Guildford to publicly abandon her now. Knowing that they had to stay together, the queen summoned the Earl of Arundel and Earl of

Pembroke to prevent her husband and mother-in-law from leaving. Later, Jane would tell Queen Mary I's officers this story, adding, 'I was compelled to act as a woman who is obliged to live on good terms with her husband; nevertheless, I was not only deluded by the duke and the Council, but maltreated by my husband and his mother.' The battle, however unpleasant, had only been domestic so far, but the new monarchy would soon have greater concerns.

At 6:00pm that evening, the Sheriff of London marched with various heralds and trumpeters to the Cross in Cheapside to proclaim that Lady Mary was unlawfully begotten, and so Jane was the new queen of England – the announcement was met with silence. Then, one young man was arrested for speaking up that Mary held the true title and should be queen. On 11 July, at 8:00am, the traitor was set on the pillory for his slip of the tongue and both his ears were cut off. On the same day, the young man's master, Sandur Onyone dwelling at St John's Head, and Master Owen, a gun-maker at London Bridge living at Ludgate, were both drowned. The message was clear: Jane was queen and no one could object.

***

As architect of the plan to gain control of the country, Dudley felt that Jane's accession had gone smoothly. He commanded London – with the Tower and armoury, the treasury, and navy – and the councillors hadn't presented any resistance. Jane's only rival for the crown was Mary Tudor, and Dudley had dispatched men to complete his plan to capture her. Despite her public favour, he couldn't see how she would be able to effectively challenge the throne: she was 37 years old, often ill, and didn't have any organised support or wealth. Her situation was so dire that her champion, Charles V, the Holy Roman Emperor, had urged his ambassador to be friendly with Dudley in order help protect her, clearly oblivious to the situation.

Most impartial observers deemed the throne to have been won by Dudley – but it was a misguided belief that didn't take into consideration the feelings of ordinary Englishmen. The general population did not stand to gain any wealth or prestige by supporting either Jane or Mary as queen, unlike the aristocratic lords, and therefore their backing was based solely on the principle of right and wrong. The public perceived that it was wrong for Jane to have ascended to the throne, and they believed that Mary should be the rightful queen. Along with the muted reception from the public, it became increasingly evident just a few days after the coronation that Dudley's hold on Jane's title was flimsy at best.

No doubt plaguing Dudley's mind was the fear that he would become the sacrificial lamb of the last unsuccessful government, just like his father had suffered during Henry VIII's reign. Having failed to capture Mary, Dudley at least tried to track her movements. He thought that if he could reach her potential supporters first, there was a chance he could sway them to his side. Dudley had prepared a letter for circulation to all the sheriffs and lieutenants in England announcing Jane's succession and ordering them to resist any appeal from Mary. But he knew the issue wouldn't be settled so easily. Such a contest would only be decided on the field of battle and, as an experienced soldier, Dudley was determined to succeed.

On 12 July, all manner of ordnance – such as guns of all sizes, and a vast quantity of cannon balls, bows, bills, spears, Moorish pikes, amour, arrows, gunpowder and stakes – was carried to the Tower by an army of men at arms. Dudley ordered a muster at Tothill Fields and offered and handsome wage of ten pence a day for those willing to fight for Queen and country. Dudley had intended to put Henry Grey, Jane's father, in charge of the attack, so that he could remain in London to personally manoeuvre the council.

The new queen would not hear of it. Overlooking the abuse and manipulation she had suffered at the hands of her parents, Jane burst into tears and begged the council to let her father remain at home, in her company. The councillors, who were already preparing to make Dudley a scapegoat for their treason, argued that since the queen was so distraught, it would be better for Dudley to command the army himself. They argued that he was such a great soldier, renowned for his defeat of the rebels in East Anglia which had kick-started his rise to fame. With no choice but to leave, Dudley stated: "Since ye think it good, I and mine will go, not doubting of your fidelity to the Queen's majesty which I leave in your custody."[9] Despite his bold words, Dudley had every reason to doubt their fidelity, yet he couldn't rebuff the request without jeopardising his standing.

On 13 July he had his personal armour delivered and appointed a retinue to meet him at Durham Place, after which he addressed the councillors for the last time. Before he rode out to destroy Mary, he commanded his councillors to send reinforcements to offer support at Newmarket. Accompanied by a number of lords and knights, gentlemen and gunners, plus many men of the guard and men of arms, Dudley left warning that if any

---

[9] Hartweg, C. (2012)

man thought to betray him or the queen, their punishment would be eternal.

"Remember", Dudley said, "the oath you took to this virtuous lady the Queen's highness, who by your and our enticement is rather of force placed therein than by her own seeking and request."[10]

The assembled lords assured him of their loyalty; one of them said, "If we should shrink from you as one that were culpable, which of us can excuse himself as guiltless? Therefore, herein your doubt is too far cast". [11]

Dudley's response? "I pray God it be so." His control of the situation was fast unravelling and even his cunning brain could not find a solution stronger than prayers.

***

On Friday, 14 July, Dudley reluctantly left to pick up his army at Cambridge, no doubt nervous of what would happen in his absence and what resistance he might meet. Although the streets were lined with villagers as the army passed through, they remained silent. "The people press to see us, but not one sayeth God speed us," [12] he

---

[10] Hanson, M. "Lady Jane Grey – Facts, Biography, Information & Portraits"
http://englishhistory.net/tudor/relative/lady-jane-grey/
February 1, 2015

[11] Hanson, M. "Lady Jane Grey – Facts, Biography, Information & Portraits"
http://englishhistory.net/tudor/relative/lady-jane-grey/
February 1, 2015

[12] Hanson, M. "Lady Jane Grey – Facts, Biography, Information & Portraits"

remarked. The council knew the reason: reports were flooding in that the wealthiest and most influential towns were now declaring Mary to be queen including Buckinghamshire, Norwich, Colchester and Oxfordshire.

Although her support was growing, Mary did not rush to claim the throne. Instead she retreated to Framlingham Castle which afforded her a stronger defence and sent word to the Emperor that she required urgent assistance if she were to avoid certain destruction. Mary need not have been so concerned, for the country was rallying behind her with her claim being declared as far away as Devon, and local land owners and tenants turning up at Framlingham to offer physical support. The six ships that Dudley had commanded to monitor the port near Mary's camp to prevent her escape defected and the crew took all the vessels and artillery to defend Mary. Dudley was even experiencing dissension in his own ranks as the men refused to fight his cause. It was plain to see the tide was turning in Mary's favour, but Dudley had to proceed if only to save face.

Back at the Tower, the in-fighting between the reluctant queen and her spouse, parents and in-laws increased. Jane spent little time with her lords during her nine days as queen and instead busied herself with the finery of the role. She ordered twenty yards of velvet, twenty-five ells of fine Holland linen cloth and thirty-three ells of coarser material for lining to create a new wardrobe and collected the royal jewels. She avoided making any political decisions and appeared to be merely biding her time until Dudley's impending failure.

---

http://englishhistory.net/tudor/relative/lady-jane-grey/
February 1, 2015

Jane did little to protect her perilous position other than issue letters instructing her loyal subjects to support a suppression of Mary's rebellion. Perhaps in a bid to distance herself from the increasingly unpopular Dudley, she signed the documents 'Jane the Queen', but the teenager must have seen the futility of the situation.

Once news reached London that the troops were deserting Dudley, the council predictably turned their back on their doomed leader in an act of self-preservation. When they attempted to leave the Tower on 16 July, they found that the main gates had been locked and the keys delivered to the queen. She had suspected one of the lords, possibly the Lord Treasurer, of trying to exit the city, but in fact two days later, on 18 July, most of her councillors escaped on the contrived pretext of visiting the French ambassador. In reality, they visited the Imperial embassy where they told Charles V's envoys that they had been bullied into acknowledging Edward VI's Device and declaring Jane as queen by Dudley. Naturally they said they had always been loyal to Mary at heart.

At around 5:00pm on Thursday, 19 July, the 'freed' councillors proclaimed Mary the new Queen of England. The people of the capital erupted into joyous celebration, with singing, dancing and feasting continuing late into the night. The foreign ambassadors were astonished, with the French envoy writing: "The atmosphere of this country and the nature of its people are so changeable that I am compelled to make my dispatches correspondingly wavering and contradictory."

Jane sat alone at supper that night, unaware what the noise outside signified. Her father, Henry Grey, interrupted her meal to tell her she had been deposed. Without fuss or protest, she helped take down the cloth of estate from above her head and sat quietly as she awaited her fate. Her father, whose greed had allowed the situation to unfold, left her side to proclaim Mary as queen at Tower Hill, before retreating to his London residence.

The frightened young girl must have longed to return to her previous incarnation as Lady Jane Grey, but she was now detained in the Tower as a prisoner. When Lady Throckmorton, one of her ladies-in-waiting, reported for duty that night, she was told her former mistress was being held in the deputy lieutenant's house – Jane's belongings had been rifled through, her money confiscated and she was accused of stealing valuables from the royal wardrobe.

Meanwhile, Dudley had been arrested and his entire family taken to the Tower; as they were marched through the streets, the crowd pelted the traitors with filth and insults. It was clear that the public had not approved of the way he so blatantly tampered with the line of succession for his own gain. The rapid fall from grace was almost unbelievable – from forcing a marriage of convenience, manipulating the line of succession and bullying the council, to desertion and pillorying in a matter of days.

Perhaps his greatest mistake was underestimating Mary, the thorn in his side. Not only was she popular in her enclave of East Anglia, but she was seen nationally as the rightful heir. By failing to capture her before pronouncing Jane's reign, Dudley effectively sealed their destinies as a rebellion was inevitable. On 3 August, Queen Mary I made her state entrance into London. Clad in purple velvet and rich jewels, she rode through the streets past cheering crowds.

Chapter Fifteen

The Waiting Game

Although captive, Jane's life improved considerably from earlier in the year as she was given books and returned to her passion of studying.

Tom was exhausted after telling such a detailed account of Jane's nine-day reign as queen, but he saw his audience was in raptures.

"So, that was it for our young ex-queen?" enquired Elliot. "Off with her head?"

John jumped in, saying, "Pretty much, although Mary deliberated for several months, presumably torn between punishing the traitors and preserving her innocent cousin. But I'm still none the wiser as to how these papers came to be found in my house."

"Why don't we look at some of the pages translated from Lady Jane Grey's journal?" suggested Tom, grateful to have a break from speaking and almost bursting with excitement. He pulled out several copies of the same text and handed them out. "The first entry picks up almost directly where I left off."

24 July 1553

It has been four days since Dudley was arrested in Cambridge. He surrendered to the authorities and on this day brought back to the Tower, this time as a prisoner. The behaviour that he has displayed proves how spineless he was and how I despised him for what he did. I watched from my window as he was escorted to the Chapel Royal. Disgusted, but not surprised by his lack of honour, I commented: "I pray God I, nor no friend of mine, die so".

He has besmirched God by his actions. In the hope of securing a pardon from the Queen, he recanted his Protestant beliefs, "by the false and erroneous teachings" of the new religion. I was told that he asked for, and was granted by my good cousin Mary, the right to attend Mass!

I fear that Mary has spent too many years in the countryside, surrounded by a Catholic household and sympathetic nobles – she doesn't see the extent of Protestantism in the vital seat of her capital and its surrounding countryside. Perhaps my blinkered cousin assumes all of England wants to return to the years before Henry VIII had decided to abandon her beloved mother and break with the Church of Rome.

"Lady Jane Grey had a point here," explained Tom. "You see, Mary had assumed that the overwhelming support she had received in reclaiming the throne, was also backing for Catholic rule in general. Her household had followed her religion and she had been surrounded by like-minded or sympathetic nobles: she had no concept of the extent to which the country was Protestant.

"Her misinformed belief was exacerbated by her most trusted political advisor – the newly-arrived Imperial ambassador, a Spaniard named Simon Renard. Charles V had sent Renard to help Mary establish her reign. Although Catholic Mass was officially illegal when Mary became queen, it was regularly celebrated at court and attended by many of the Privy Council who willingly traded their religious leanings. When pushed by Renard to take direct action to change the country's religion, Mary advised that she would not, 'compel or constrain other men's consciences'. She hoped that her patience would allow her subjects to open their hearts and find the truth, returning to her religion themselves.

"But going back to Lady Jane, Renard's counsel to Mary was to enforce moderate punishment upon her and the traitors who had supported her claim. He was under guidance from Charles that Mary should not be to be too cruel as to hurt her reputation, but she must be seen to take action. However, Renard complained to his master that Mary could not be drawn to commit Lady Jane Grey to death. As you said John, Mary believed her cousin was innocent in the plot. She saw that her cousin had no desire to be queen, had been forced into the position by Dudley and posed no further threat. On that basis, Mary could not condemn an innocent young girl.

"Renard commended Mary for her trusting nature, but advised her that kindness could easily be destroyed by dishonesty. He warned that the girl who had worn the crown for nine days could be used as a symbol for rebellion. In the meantime, no one was speaking up for poor old Jane."

3 August 1553

I have heard that Mary is back in London. I wrote to her for the witness of my innocence and the disburdening of my conscience. I realise that no one will intercede on my behalf, so I felt obliged to describe the string of events since my forced marriage to Guildford Dudley. I admitted that I was wrong to accept the crown, but impressed on her that I was merely relying on the advice of others and doing the bidding of my elders.

I appealed to my cousin's goodness and clemency so that Mary may realise that I might have taken upon me that of which I was not worthy, yet no one can ever say either that I sought it.... or that I was pleased with it. I haven't heard from her yet. While I am being treated well, I am curious as to what and when will be my sentence.

"Dudley's fate however," continued Tom as he handed out more text, "was obvious and inevitable."

22 August 1553

I have heard word today that John Dudley is to be executed. There was little doubting the decision of the court and in fact he was sentenced to die yesterday. I understand that he had sent out a last desperate appeal to Lord Arundel for his intercession. Among other things that he hath said was the old proverb that a living dog is better than a dead lion. Apparently he then proposed to spend his days in Queen Mary I's honourable service, as he had done for both her father and brother. Given how he had behaved towards my cousin, Mary, and myself, there was little chance, despite her grace and mercy, of any change in his fate.

Finally, he announced that he wanted to be reconciled to the Catholic faith. I don't know if he hoped to avert his own death by appealing to the queen's religion, or whether he genuinely wished to convert. I suspect it was the former, but either way his execution was delayed for one day while he made his peace with God.

He was escorted – with his son and William Parr – to St Peter ad Vincula, the church within the Tower of London grounds. There, he attended mass and, upon receiving the sacrament, Dudley addressed the crowd. An eyewitness told me he said:

"My masters, I let you all to understand that I do most faithfully believe this is the very right and true way, out of the which true religion you and I have been seduced these sixteen years past, by the false and erroneous preaching of the new preachers.... And I do believe the holy sacrament here most assuredly to be our Saviour and Redeemer Jesus Christ and this I pray you all to testify and pray for me."[13]

So at nine o'clock this morning, John Dudley was executed for treason at Tower Hill before a great crowd of spectators.

I didn't feel any sense of loss or feeling, despite the fact I was told that he has gone out of his way to exonerate me from having aspired to take the crown. Apparently he stated that I had been, "enticed and forced and made to accept it". No doubt a combination of his honesty at the end and Mary's clemency has saved my neck presently. For now, I am grateful to simply remain a prisoner.

"By this point, Jane realised she was probably safe from imminent death," continued Tom, "and while she was still in the Tower, she was treated with more respect than the average prisoner. She had a staff of four: two attendant ladies, Mrs Tylney and Mrs Jacob, one

---

[13] Adams, S. (ed.) (1995)

manservant, and her nurse and lifelong companion, Mrs Ellen, each paid 20 shillings a week by the government.

"Although captive, Jane's life improved considerably from earlier in the year as she was given books and allowed to return to her passion of studying. She was able to take a stroll in the Queen's garden when she desired and she enjoyed spending time with the gentleman gaoler, Nathaniel Partridge, and his wife who showed her kindness. Moreover, she no longer had to deal with her dreadful parents or in-laws, none of whom was making any attempt to save her. Mary not only refused to sentence her cousin, but she also spoke of the precautions she would set in place when Jane was eventually awarded her liberty. Renard was not amused."

29 August 1553

We dined at No. 5 Tower Green. I was in high spirits tonight. We were joined by Rowland Lea, an official of the Royal Mint who was also living in the same precinct. He was, I believe a friend of the Gentleman Partridge, my gaoler. I had decided to dine with the family that evening and I was given the place of honour at the board's end.

I opened the conversation by saying that Master Partridge, and his friend Mr Lea, may remain covered and allowed them to put back on their caps. I proposed a toast to their good health and bade them a hearty welcome. Grateful for being free to have such moments, I also gave thanks to the Queen's Majesty and beseeched God that long may she continue, and He should send His bountiful grace upon her.

Eager for news from outside, I enquired whether or not they had Mass in London. Lea answered me directly, "Yes, in some places".

I commented that it may be so, but asked if he did not find strange the sudden conversion of the late Duke of Northumberland, my father-in-law John Dudley – who would have thought he would have so done?

To which Partridge answered, "Perchance he thereby hoped to have had his pardon."

"Pardon!" I exclaimed, and here I can recall my words quite clearly: "He hath brought me and our stock in most miserable calamity and misery by his exceeding ambition. He should receive no pardon. What man is there living, I pray you, that would hope of life after his being so hatred and evil spoken of by the commons? Who was the judge that he should hope for pardon, whose life was odious to all men? Like as his life was wicked and full of dissimulation, so was his end thereafter.

"He hoped for life by turning his religion? Though other men be of that opinion, I utterly am not. Should I, who am so young, and in my few years, forsake my faith for the love of life? Nay, God forbid! But God be merciful to us. For he sayeth, Whoso denyeth Me before men, I will not know him in My Father's kingdom."

Perhaps I had spoken too long and with a tone too serious for a dinner, but with this and such similar talk, the meal passed away. I do recall Lea thanking me and addressing me as Lady Jane, to which I replied, "I thank you. You are welcome." I too thanked Partridge for bringing such a fine gentleman to dinner.

Partridge answered, "Madam, we were somewhat bold, not knowing that your ladyship dined below until we found your ladyship there." I then retired to transcribe the conversations of the evening and heard Partridge's guest hurrying back to his lodging within the Tower.

"Woah, Jane really didn't like Dudley then," commented Elliot.

"You can hardly blame her!" defended Alice.

"Yes, her intense hatred of Dudley is painfully evident in this passage, not to mention her fanatical religious convictions. But the latter is well documented. There's a letter she wrote to Dr Harding, her first tutor and a former chaplain at her parents' home of Bradgate, when she learnt that he too had joined other Protestant chaplains in renouncing their faith and converting back to Catholicism. Jane let him know the extent of her disgust and commented on his appalling cowardice. Here is a translation of one of the loose-leaf letters we found to Harding:

I cannot but marvel at thee and lament thy case, who seemed sometime to be the lively member of Christ, but now the deformed imp of the devil; sometime the beautiful temple of God, but now the stinking and filthy kennel of Satan; sometime the unspotted spouse of Christ, but now the unshamefaced paramour of Antichrist; sometime my faithful brother, but now a stranger and apostate; sometime a stout Christian soldier, but now a cowardly runaway. Yea, when I consider these things, I cannot but speak to thee, and cry out upon thee, thou seed of Satan.

Oh wretched and unhappy man, what art thou but dust and ashes? And wilt thou resist thy Maker that fashioned thee and framed thee?... Wilt thou refuse the true God, and worship the invention of man, the golden calf, the whore of Babylon, the Romish religion, the abominable idol, the most wicked mass?'[14]

---

[14] Adams, S. (ed) (2002)

"We all knew she was pious," elaborated Tom, "but this shows her to be exceptionally self-righteous and religiously intolerant. In fact, she was more like Mary than most people realised – both were outspoken, honest and passionate about their religion, to the point of being rude about others."

5 September 1553

The summer has been warm and pleasant and I have been permitted to walk, accompanied by the Gentleman's wife, through the grounds to have some air. The walks we took along the parapet, feeling the warmth of the summer sun on my face, were quite lovely. Guildford, I understand, wanted to join me, but I couldn't think of anything more ghastly. I have seen him a few times but his manner alone depresses me. I never did seek his presence and now more than ever, given our circumstances and that of his father, did I not want his company.

He says that we are a proper husband and wife and should be together, but both he and I know that not to be true. He had tried to force himself upon me, but I resisted with a strength that quite surprised me as he is much bigger and stronger than I. Still, once he had completely overpowered me and quite pinned me to the floor like a butterfly to a board for display, it was he who was unable to act despite his effort. He let me go and sobbed in the corner like a scolded child. I did rather goad him by saying that perhaps he needed his father to help him. Rather than retort or come at me he simply sobbed more. I did wonder whether he preferred the company of boys, given the manner in which he jested with his male courtiers.

Queen Mary had left the Tower herself for Richmond in August. I knew this because it was suddenly very quiet and actually quite peaceful. For the whole summer I was left in a rather strange state, imprisoned but feeling quite content to continue with my studies away from all the noise and distraction. Though it has been five years since her death I still miss Queen Catherine, she was the mother with whom I wished I had been blessed. I'm sure that she would have used her wisdom to sort out this most awful of messes in which we all find ourselves.

1 October 1553

Today I learned the news of Queen Mary I's coronation following a procession yesterday. They say it was a lavish two-day event. I am told she looked resplendent in a purple gown with ermine edges. She wore a circlet of gold and jewels on her head that was so valuable and heavy to bear.

Yesterday she travelled by carriage to London, flanked by lords, bishops and knights, as well as members of the Privy Council and other senior nobles. In her procession, she gave a carriage to her sister, Princess Elizabeth, and Anne of Cleves, who had suffered the same fate of divorce by Henry VIII as Mary's own mother. The procession route was lined by well-wishers and performers, putting on great displays for her.

When Mary reached the city, she was welcomed by the Recorder of London in a speech promising the loyalty of her subjects in the country's capital, then handed a gold thread purse bearing one thousand gold coins.

Today, Mary travelled by barge on the River Thames to the old Whitehall Palace. At eleven o'clock this morning, the queen entered the Abbey dressed in the traditional garb for a male monarch: the usual state robes of crimson velvet. The ceremony followed the typical format, with Mary prostrating herself before the altar on a velvet cushion while prayers were said over her, before she took her oath.

Afterwards, Mary changed into a petticoat of purple velvet before being anointed by Stephen Gardner, the Bishop of Winchester, with holy oil on her shoulders, breast, forehead and temples. Finally, Mary received the sword, the sceptre and orbs once back in her robes of state, and was crowned with the Imperial Crown from Edward the Confessor, and then a custom-made one of her own.

I absorbed all this news from Partridge's wife, not with any jealousy, but warm interest and best wishes for my cousin. I marvelled at how the welcome differed to Dudley's rushed attempt at my own coronation: his plan was doomed from the start.

"While Mary was busy enjoying her coronation, she continued her policy of clemency and was seen to be awarding fines instead of execution," explained Tom to help the others understand the next journal entry. "Renard was displeased, but it took the public view of Mary's weakened authority to prompt her to take action. She had to be seen to be taking action, so she called for a trial of Dudley's four sons and Jane."

14 November 1553

The summer and autumn have passed pleasantly enough, for although I have been imprisoned I have been treated fairly and been afforded time for my studies and correspondence. Today, however, is finally the day of my trial. Judgement Day.

I have been waiting for this moment since September when my cousin announced there would be a trial for myself and the Dudley men. I dressed myself with much thought and chose a suitably sober outfit for the occasion: a black cloth gown, a black cape trimmed with velvet and a black French hood, also trimmed with velvet. I hung a black velvet bound prayer book at my girdle and held a book of prayers open in my hands. Naturally I was attended by my two ladies, Mrs Tylney and Mrs Jacob, as I walked behind Guildford to London's Guild Hall.

Of course, the proceedings were a mere formality as we all pleaded guilty to the charge of high treason, it was just a matter of finding out our sentences: the men would be hung, drawn, and quartered, while I was told I would be burnt or beheaded at the Queen's pleasure. As we walked back to the Tower, the executioner turned the edge of his axe towards us so that onlookers could know we were condemned.

How wretched I felt to be caught up with the Dudleys, while the rest of my own family had escaped almost without penance. My father paid a hefty fine, but was given a general pardon and returned to court. My mother I am told is Queen Mary's favourite lady and my sisters, Catherine and Mary, are her ladies-in-waiting. Some gossips had suggested that given my mother's favour in court, I might be pardoned and released, but not according to today's events.

"Mary's clemency and reluctance to execute her cousin is important in this tale," explained Tom, when the trio had finished reading, "as in fact she had no real intention of executing Jane. But we need to understand a bit more about her to appreciate why she acted as she did… particularly in light of the new information Jane’s journal reveals.”

Chapter Sixteen

There's Something About Mary

Mary's success was popular with the people and friends of the late administration hastened to make their peace once they saw that resistance was futile and dutifully fell in line.

The trio were struggling to keep up with all the history they were hearing and trying to decipher what new information the journal had revealed. John, who was the most au fait with the period, challenged this point.

"Sorry Tom, I'm not sure if I've missed something, but other than recording the relatively lenient conditions in which Lady Jane was 'imprisoned', I'm not sure we've heard anything we didn't know already?"

"Patience, my dear fellow. Patience," replied Tom, feeling supercilious. Then, as promised, he detailed a potted history of Mary's ascension to the throne and her primary drivers at the time of Jane's sentencing. He explained that Mary was the eldest daughter of the second Tudor King, the infamous Henry VIII, and the only surviving child from his first, wife, the devoutly Catholic Catherine of Aragon. Mary really was her mother's daughter and followed the faith with the same degree of diligence and devotion. Her formative years were dominated by religious role models, such as the king's advisor, Cardinal Wolsey, who was also her godfather. Growing up, she counted amongst her most intimate friends, Cardinal Reginald Pole and his mother, Margaret Pole (nee Plantagenet), also known as the Countess of Salisbury and Mary's godmother. What happened to the Countess may have had a significant bearing on the manner in which Mary conducted herself throughout her life.

Born Lady Margaret Plantagenet, at Farleigh Hungerford Castle in Somerset, she was the only surviving daughter of the first Duke of Clarence and the former Lady Isabella Neville, the elder daughter of the Earl of Warwick and Anne Neville, who had inherited the Earldom of Warwick. When Margaret was three, her mother and her youngest brother died, and her father was executed the following year for treason. Margaret and her remaining brother would have held a potential claim to the throne, but were debarred due to their father's attainder. When their uncle assumed the throne as Richard III, the children were kept at a castle in Yorkshire, and Margaret was later given to the king's cousin, Sir Richard Pole, in marriage.

Margaret was widowed with five children, but found herself a lady-in-waiting to Catherine of Aragon. When some of her family's land was reinstated, she managed it well and became the fifth richest peer in England, as well as a patron of the renaissance. Her favour in court was intermittent, but in 1520 she was appointed godmother and sponsor-in-confirmation for Princess Mary, later becoming Governess of the child and her household. As the years passed there was talk of a marriage between

Margaret's young charge and her second son, Reginald. However, the young lad spoke boldly, some may say foolishly, about King Henry's impending divorce, and left England shortly afterwards in some disgrace.

Princess Mary was cast as illegitimate when King Henry divorced Catherine to marry Anne Boleyn in 1533. Margaret defended her charge's claim to the throne, but was removed from her post for her trouble. She begged to be allowed to follow and serve Mary at her own expense, and finally returned to court following the demise of Anne.

Margaret's downfall came when her son Reginald sent King Henry a copy of his published treaties, *Pro ecclesiastic unitatis defensive*, which, although dressed up as theology, essentially denounced the King's behaviour and policies. King Henry VIII was enraged and, despite a letter from Margaret reproving her son, he determined that the family would pay for the insubordination. Two of Margaret's sons and a number of other relatives were arrested on treason, committed to the Tower and, with the exception of her youngest son, Geoffrey, were executed.

Ten days after the arrest of her sons, Margaret was detained and questioned, despite her age. Her interrogators reported to Cromwell that, although they had travailed with her' for many hours, she would 'nothing utter'. They were forced to conclude that either her sons had not made her 'privy nor participant' to their treason, or else she was 'the most arrant traitress that ever lived'.

Margaret was committed to Cowdray House and subjected to all manner of indignities. Cromwell robbed her of her titles, produced a white silk tunic found in one of her coffers, which was embroidered on the back with the Five Sacred Wounds, believed to refer to the five piercing wounds that were suffered during the crucifixion of Jesus, and she was 'attainted to die by Act of Parliament'. She was removed to the Tower of London and held there for nearly two years, during which time she was 'tormented by the severity of the weather and insufficient clothing'.

Given her important role in Princess Mary's life, the words found carved into Margaret's cell wall must have resonated when she took the throne as Queen Mary:

I am no traitor, no, not I!
My faithfulness stands fast and so,
Towards the block I shall not go!
Nor make one step, as you shall see;
Christ in Thy Mercy, save Thou me!

On the morning of 27 May 1541, Margaret was told she was to die within the hour. As she was of noble birth, she was not executed before the populace, though there were still about 150 witnesses. Yet she was executed with appalling barbarity: Lady Margaret, who was 67 years old, frail and ill, was dragged to the block and forced when she refused to lay her head down. One account tells how the inexperienced executioner's first blow made a deep gash in her shoulder rather than her neck; a further ten blows were required to complete the execution.

Some see King Henry's eventual execution of Lady Margaret as the continuation of his father's programme to eliminate possible contenders for the throne: she was among the last of the Plantagenets remaining alive after the War of the Roses.

These events serve to highlight the paranoid, fickle and brutal world in which Princess Mary and her siblings existed. Despite this, her contemporaries report that in her youth, Mary did not lack charm, was modest by nature, affectionate and kindly. Like all Tudor princesses, she was well educated, speaking Latin, French, and Spanish, and was an accomplished musician. Mary was initially recognised as heir to the throne and many suitors had been proposed. However, when her father became determined to divorce her mother, Mary fell from favour. In 1531, to their great mutual grief, mother and daughter were forcibly separated and the young girl was stripped of her title.

During Anne Boleyn's brief reign as queen, Mary suffered the harshest treatment with rumours abounding that she and her mother would end up in the gallows. After the death of her mother in January 1536, and her step-mother a few months later, Jane Seymour, the new Queen, befriended her husband's eldest daughter.

Under strong pressure from the still-powerful Cromwell, Mary signed (without reading) a formal 'submission', in which she begged pardon of the King whom she had, 'obstinately and disobediently offended', renounced 'the Bishop of Rome's pretended authority', and acknowledged the marriage between her father and mother to have been contrary to the Law of God.

Slowly, but surely, Mary returned to favour and, after King Henry VIII's marriage to his sixth wife, Catherine Parr, the princess' position was much improved: she was restored to court and named in her father's will as second in line to the throne after her younger brother, Edward.

When King Henry VIII eventually died, it was inevitable that Mary should retire into comparative obscurity as the regency jostled for supremacy with the young king. In the main, she hid herself away at her manors of Hunsdon, Kenninghall and Newhall. When her

Protestant brother prohibited the celebration of Mass, she, perhaps unwisely, wrote to the Council and appealed to the Holy Roman Emperor. Ruffling a few feathers, at one time it seemed as if King Charles V of Spain would declare war with England over the issue, however Mary was able to remain outwardly friendly with her brother, and occasionally paid him visits of state. Throughout the episode, Mary remained firm and defiant, at least with regards to the religious observances followed in her own household.

Tom reminded his audience that when the teenage king died on 6 July 1553, the news was kept from Mary for several days, but on hearing the news and learning of Dudley's plot to capture her and crown Lady Jane Grey, Mary acted promptly and decisively, setting up her standard at Framlingham. By 19 July, Mary had been proclaimed Queen in London and a few days later Dudley was arrested.

Mary's success was popular with the people and friends of the late administration hastened to make their peace once they saw that resistance was futile, dutifully falling in line. Her own inclinations, due to her good nature and perhaps Lady Margaret's plight, were in favour of clemency, but in deference to her advisers, she consented to the execution of the Dudley, along with two of his followers.

Her coronation was a popular event spanning two days over the end of September and beginning of October 1553, ending in great pomp at Westminster. Conversely, her first few acts were less well received. The new queen was determined to stamp out Protestantism and reintroduce Catholicism; she embraced obedience to papal authority and negotiations had already been opened with the Holy See (enthronement ceremony for the

Bishops of Rome) to put England back on the road to Catholicism.

To complete this brief account of a particularly turbulent time in English history, the restoration of the old religion went on vigorously: the altars were re-established, the married clergy were deprived, High Mass was sung at St. Paul's, and new bishops were consecrated according to the ancient ritual. The wealth of religious legislative activity stirred the passions of the more fervent Reformers and they devoted increased efforts against the pope. Mary and her advisers concluded that religious peace was impossible unless these fanatics were silenced, and so they enforced the repealed penalties for heresy.

What motivated Mary to enact the deplorable severities which followed is unclear. It may have been part revenge for the atrocities carried out by the Protestant reformers, King Henry VIII and King Edward VI, or simply a misguided zeal for peace in her beloved Church, given the context of the time. Whatever the reason, Mary has her place in history as being principally responsible for the death of 277 people, barbarically burned to death, in less than four years. Reports of the time say that at prominent Protestant Bishop Cranmer's burning, young sapling wood was used that would burn less vigorously to enable a slow and painful death, so vengeance undoubtedly played its part in her actions.

***

It was not just the return to Catholicism which displeased the public, for Mary's choice of husband also caused great unrest. Owing partly to the fact that Queen Mary I was heavily influenced by the Spanish ambassador, Renard, she had made up her mind to marry Philip, soon-to-be king of Spain, but the complexities of Mary Tudor's remarkably unpopular decision to marry the 26-year-old widower are many.

No woman had ruled England in their own right before, and so it was expected that Mary would marry in order to have a king for support and guidance. The English public favoured a union with Edward Courtenay, the great-grandson of Edward IV and the last of the Plantagenets. He was young, good-looking, and charming, and came from noble lineage which meant that he had spent his first decade in close proximity with the royal household. However, his father's involvement in the Exeter Conspiracy led him to spend his teenage years in prison, not being released as he was deemed a direct threat to King Henry VIII as the likely heir to the House of York.

Edward VI had shown leniency to many prisoners when he took the crown, but Courtenay was not one of them. Mary, on the other hand, was more sympathetic, releasing him from the Tower and restoring both Edward and his mother to royal grace. Indicative of her caring nature, this act was also no doubt to repay Edward's family when they had supported her mother, Catherine of Aragon, during the great divorce. However, while she bestowed many kindnesses on the family, she made it perfectly clear that she would not marry Edward.

Mary had always turned to her mother's Spanish family for advice and support, particularly after she was disinherited by her father, and she continued to do so when she became queen. Her cousin, Charles V, suggested she marry Philip of Spain – not only was he an eligible prince and heir apparent to vast sections of continental Europe and territories in the new world, but he was also the grandson of her aunt. As part of the marriage negotiations, Charles ceded additional land to Philip and sent Mary a portrait of his son by way of introduction.

Deeply religious and a chaste maiden of nearly 40, Mary had essentially spent her adulthood alone and was fearful of marriage to a worldly-wise widow a decade her junior. Renard glossed over the fact that Philip's motives for marriage were purely political and driven by power – for he would enjoy equal titles and honours as his wife – and assured Mary that Philip would be delighted to marry her. To seal the deal, he reminded her that they would have children, thus providing England with a Catholic future. Succession was such a weight to bear that the queen agreed to the marriage, if only to continue leading her subjects down her perceived path of righteousness after she passed. The engagement was announced in October 1553.

The English public did not want Mary to wed a Spaniard for the same reason that King Edward VI had excluded her from succession – she was past middle-age and would probably bear no children, therefore leaving the throne to a foreign Catholic husband and exposing England to becoming yet another state of the Imperial Empire. The queen faced a hostile reaction at home, from patriots saying she should have married an Englishman, from Protestants fearing a Catholic overthrow and from the King of France who feared a Spanish-led war with England. Rumours ran rife – from a Spanish invasion to immediate war – fuelled by Protestant propagandists and the French ambassador. Mary's advisors were ineffectual and her simultaneous promotion of Catholicism did little to calm the nation: word soon reached London of numerous uprisings in the countryside led by Carew in Devonshire, Crofts in Wales, Grey in Leicestershire and Wyatt in Kent.

The rebellions were raised under the guise of opposition to the Spanish alliance, but were notably all led by Protestants and the aim was to overthrow Mary in favour of her half-sister, Elizabeth, who they intended would marry Edward Courtenay. The rebels had planned four separate uprisings, each in their respective county, converging in London on 18 March 1554, when Prince Philip was due to arrive in England. Renard suspected such a plot and arrested Courtenay for questioning and he betrayed them, revealing the plans.

The conspirators were forced into premature action, but most of them failed to raise an army and dispersed. Wyatt received the greatest support in Kent and pressed on with the attempted coup, amassing an army of some 4,000 men. For a few days it seemed as though the crown may capitulate to the pressure from the rebels, but Wyatt's outrageous demands turned London against him. Mary personally addressed her citizens from the Guildhall, against the advice of the Council who feared for her safety, and her forthright and rousing speech rallied the troops to crush the uprising.

Mary shut London's bridges to prevent Wyatt's army entering, but refused to let the Tower guns be fired on the traitors, lest the innocent citizens of Southwark be harmed in crossfire. The rebels eventually surrendered, but not without making it clear that the queen's religion and foreign union were deeply divisive. While the action did not change Mary's plans to marry Philip, it did seal the fate of Lady Jane Grey.

Renard, who had foiled the plot, suggested that neither the queen nor Prince Philip would be safe from further uprisings unless the rebels were dealt with harshly. While Wyatt had instigated the uprising, Henry Grey had also tried to raise an army against the Spanish marriage.

Although Grey had gained little support, his intention had been to lead his army from the midland shires to London. Rumours abounded that he had once again proclaimed his daughter, Lady Jane Grey, as queen during his ride. Although this was probably untrue, it planted enough concern in the minds of Mary's advisors. There was no doubting that Jane was innocent – she was locked up in the Tower – but she had once been queen and would always be inextricably linked to any Protestant plot. Therefore, she was deemed a danger.

Renard and Mary's council inevitably agreed that the queen must execute Lady Jane Grey to remove any future threat to her reign. As a direct result of the Wyatt rebellion, not to mention her father's involvement, the suspended sentence on Lady Jane Grey was revoked and she was condemned to die immediately.

The date of the execution was set for Friday, 9 February 1554.

Elizabeth, who was also implicated in the rebellion, was imprisoned for a while, but later shown mercy. Mary tried one last time to save her cousin's soul as she was so reluctant to kill the young girl. John Feckenham, Dean of St Paul's, was sent to visit Jane and was given a few days to persuade her to convert to the Catholic faith. Although Jane had enjoyed company and the opportunity to study in the Tower, she had been deprived of intellectual and theological debate and so relished the prospect of deliberating matters with Feckenham. Rather than acquiescing, she defiantly rebutted each of his arguments with her own beliefs, apparently enjoying this last chance to expound on her precious faith.

After hours of discussion, she remained resolutely Protestant and therefore condemned to die. She had however come to like Feckenham very much and so she accepted his offer to accompany her to the scaffold. There, she promised to "pray God in the bowels of his mercy to send you his Holy Spirit; for he hath given you his great gift of utterance, if it pleased him also to open the eyes of your heart."[15]

Jane Grey possessed the committed idealism of a religious fanatic. While her cousin Mary never questioned her own passionate Catholicism, Jane did review her Protestant faith, but the quest for spiritual meaning only reinforced her already strong convictions. Had she remained queen, there is every possibility she would have oppressed Catholics with the same energy that Mary persecuted Protestants, which earned the latter the nickname Bloody Mary. Instead, Jane's fate was to be executed and later celebrated as a Protestant martyr, the greatest sacrificial lamb of Mary's misguided policies.

In many ways, the power and influence of religion over Mary made her a contradiction, given the clemency and generosity she uniformly demonstrated in other areas of her life. Mary's good qualities, of which there were many, were lost over the years among the headlines of so many executions. Ultimately, she was a disappointed woman, perhaps one of the most tragic in English history. However, if it was known that she had kept a secret to the grave, history may have viewed her in a kinder light.

---

[15] Plowden, A. (2004)

Chapter Seventeen

I Pray You Dispatch Me Quickly

If justice be done with my body, my soul will find mercy with God I will give pain to my body for its sins, but the soul will be justified before God.

After a brief recap on Queen Mary I, Tom refocused his audience's attention to the fate of Lady Jane Grey with more journal entries, affording him another pause in story-telling.

26 January 1554

I have heard news of a number of Protestant uprisings. The one which caught my attention was the Wyatt Rebellion, quashed yesterday. Time will tell if the rumours I heard are correct, but the information I received is as follows: a Protestant rebellion was instigated by a number of conspirators, keen to depose Queen Mary and instate the Protestant Princess Elizabeth as new queen. The mastermind behind the scheme was Sir Thomas Wyatt, although other nobles have been implicated in aborted uprisings, including my father, who I also understand to be missing.

"It was this uprising that effectively sealed Jane's fate," Tom reminded the trio, "even though she had nothing to do with it. Jane's father, Henry Grey, the Duke of Suffolk, and his two brothers joined the rebellion, which caused the government to conclude the verdict against Jane and Guildford, similarly sealing the fate of Henry and his brother."

10 February 1554

I have been told that my father has been arrested and is now imprisoned too in the Tower. He has proved himself to be more of a fool than even I could have imagined. How did he ever think that this would end in a good way?

Seven months have passed since the king died on 6 July, and that fateful day on 9 July when I was told that I was queen. I neither wanted nor sought this destiny. I was not only deluded by the Duke and the Council, but maltreated by my husband and his mother, and disowned and betrayed by my Godless parents. I know not how my short life will be remembered in history, if at all. While I bear no malice to those who so hurt me, I hope the record stands correct at the duplicitous treatment I have borne. Yet I care not what mortal men think of the situation, for I am at ease knowing that only He knows the truth. He alone will cast the final judgement and I know in my heart that I will pass the test. I must trust Him to pass the correct sentence on those who betray Him.

My final day has nearly come to pass, so I am undertaking some correspondence. This is what I have written to my father:

Although it hath pleased God to hasten my death by you, by whom my life should rather have been lengthened, yet can I patiently take it, that I yield God more hearty thanks for shortening my woeful days, than if all the world had been given unto my possession, with life lengthened at my own will. And albeit, I am well assured of your impatient dolours redoubled many ways, both in bewailing your own woe and especially, as I am informed, my woeful estate; yet, my dear father, if I may without offense rejoice in my own mishap, herein I account myself blessed, that washing my hands with the innocency of my face, my guiltless blood may cry before the Lord, Mercy to the innocent... In taking [the crown] upon me, I seemed to consent and therein grievously offended the Queen and her laws... And thus, good father, I have opened unto you the state in which I presently stand, my death at hand, although to you it may seem woeful, yet to me, there is nothing more welcome than from this vale of misery to aspire to that heavenly throne of all joy and pleasure, with Christ our Saviour.

Your obedient daughter 'til death, Jane Dudley. [16]

I have also penned a farewell to my dear sister Catherine, to reassure her that she must not worry about

---

[16] Hanson, M. "The executions of Lady Jane Grey & Lord Guildford Dudley, 1554" http://englishhistory.net/tudor/executions-of-lady-jane-grey-lord-guildford-dudley/ February 8, 2015

me and that I am at peace knowing I will be looked after in my onward journey.

I have sent you, good sister Catherine, a book which, although it be not outwardly trimmed with gold, yet inwardly it is more worth than precious stones. It is the book, dear sister, of the laws of the lord: It is His Testament and Last Will, which He bequeathed unto us wretches, which shall lead you to the path of eternal joy, and if you, with a good mind read it, and with an earnest desire, follow it shall bring you to an immortal and everlasting life.

It will teach you to live and learn you to die... [the book] shall win you more than you should have gained by the possession of your woeful father's lands, for as if God prospered him, you shall inherit his lands... [the contents contain] such riches as neither the covetous shall withdraw from you, neither the thief shall steal, neither let the moth corrupt... And as touching my death, rejoice as I do and consider that I shall be delivered of this corruption and put on incorruption, for as I am assured that I shall for losing of a mortal life, find an immortal felicity. Pray God grant you and send you his grace to live in the love...

Farewell good sister, put only your trust in God, who only must uphold you,

Your loving sister, Jane Dudley [17]

11 February 1554

It is another cold day outside. I can see a mist sitting on the water and most of London from my view though

[17] Lady Jane Grey Reference Guide citing Ives, E. (2009)

the slit window is shrouded in a fog so murky, it is difficult to make out any of the buildings in the distance.

I have very much enjoyed my time spent with Mr Feckenham over the last two days and our discussions have engaged my mind once more. He made some emotive arguments, ones which I can understand might sway folk of a weaker disposition than I. Someone like the treacherous Dudley, no doubt, could be persuaded that Catholicism might hold the answer to redemption. But I am fortunate enough to know that my learnings are correct. I thank the Lord that I know the truth in my heart and have no need to change my beliefs in exchange for my life. For what life would I lead if I were untrue to Him. None that I would want.

It is unfortunate that cousin Mary deems me to be a threat, for I have no desire upon her crown. She is most welcome to it and all the trappings of power. So I accept her decision and will not bargain for my life. Certainly no one else feels that it is worthwhile.

I have written to Mr Feckenham to show my appreciation of his time spent with me. Although we have different beliefs, I know that someday he will understand mine to be the truth.

I think that at the supper I neither receive flesh nor blood, but bread and wine; which bread when it is broken, and the wine when it is drunken, put me in remembrance how that for my sins the body of Christ was broken, and his blood shed on the cross... I ground my faith upon God's word, and not upon the church. The faith of the church must be tried by God's word, and not God's word by the church; neither yet my faith.[18]

Words written and then re-read provide great comfort to me and I have written this entry in my prayer book:

The Lord comfort your Grace and that in His word wherein all creatures only are to be comforted. And though it hath pleased God to take two of your children, yet think not, I most humbly beseech your Grace, that you have lost them. But trust that we, by leaving this mortal life, have won an immortal life. And I, as for my part, as I have honoured your Grace in this life, will pray for you in another life.

Your Grace's humble daughter, Jane Dudley [19]

If justice be done with my body, my soul will find mercy with God I will give pain to my body for its sins, but the soul will be justified before God. If my faults deserve punishment, my youth at least, and my imprudence, were worthy of excuse; God and posterity will show me favour. [20]

---

[18] Lady Jane Grey Reference Guide citing Nicolas, N.H.N. (1825)

[19] Ives, E. (2009) pp. 267, 268

[20] Ives, E. (2009) pp. 268-70

Chapter Eighteen

Two People, One Coat

...the voices in the tower echoed around the harsh stone walls and the sound of footsteps on the solid stairs signalled the regular rounds of activity.

"This next entry is the exciting one," beamed Tom, pleased as punch.

"Is this it?" enquired John. "Because I can't take any more of the slow reveal. You're going to tell us next that Mary was actually a peasant who dressed as the queen, taking her place after secretly stealing into the palace and murdering the real Queen Mary, and throwing her corpse down the nearest well, making some unknown commoner now the real heir to the English throne!"

There was a long pause. Elliot and Alice shifted uncomfortably, wondering if John had pushed Tom too far. "What is it, Tom?" asked Alice sweetly, trying to soften the mood that she sensed had been soured. But when Tom spoke, the trio were in for a big surprise.

"Whether that was a lucky guess, or you have great powers of intuition, your jest was actually pretty close,

John. I'll use a metaphor: you're in the right town, but on the wrong street.

"Now remember, Jane was queen for nine days, from 10 to 19 July 1553. She was sixteen, being born sometime in October 1537, the exact date is unknown. She is believed to have died at the executioners block on 12 February 1554. Records tell us that Jane's remains were buried in the Church of St. Peter ad Vincula, in the Tower of London." Tom took a sip of his drink before continuing while the others sat in anticipatory silence.

"See what you make of this then," he said handing over another scroll of paper, like a teacher at a school prize-giving.

11 February 1554

Darkness had descended hours earlier and the street commotion that I could hear through the slit that passed for a window had died to a hush. Still, the voices in the tower echoed around the harsh stone walls and the sound of footsteps on the solid stairs signalled the regular rounds of activity. Shouts across the courtyard below broke the intermittent quiet, but the stillness of the night enveloped me once more.

Someone was approaching the door to my cell – I could tell because the narrow corridor reverberated an echo which unintentionally announced even the most discreet of visitors. I stayed stock-still as a key jangled in the lock. A shaft of light was the first to enter the room as the heavy wooden door creaked on its hinges. Expecting no guests or food, I was intrigued by this irregular intrusion.

Two dark figures entered the room, their identity concealed by the dancing shadows of my lone candle which provided the only illumination. I recognised one of the silhouettes standing in front of me in an instant and felt my knees buckle at the knowledge. Beyond them, at the entrance to my prison, stood two sizeable guards with their backs to me; they clearly had no intention of being involved.

We stood for a moment in an uneasy silence, but it was not my place to speak. The smaller of the two visitors made the slightest gesture of a nod to me, but kept her head down. The petite form started coughing and raised a doll-like hand to her mouth to expectorate something into the fold of a light-coloured piece of cotton. Leaning closer and lifting my candle a fraction, I could see a stain of what looked like blood in the handkerchief, but I dared not move any further.

Anticipation filled the cold chamber and hung stagnant in the musty air. I bowed my head and mentally recited a prayer, unaware that my lips were mouthing each word. I waited for the familiar character to speak, knowing that she would when ready.

“You will die tomorrow,” she commanded in a clipped and assured tone. “Are you ready to make your peace with God and save your soul for eternity?”

Out of respect for my God I completed the prayer in my head, and was about to form a verbal response when I was halted by the stranger. “I am, your majesty,” came the faint reply. “My family are forever indebted to you for your kindness, to end my suffering and allow my soul to enter the Kingdom of Heaven on your bidding.”

“Then we must leave, for we have stayed too long already.”

The tiny creature, a girl of no more than early teenage years, kept her eyes down and shrugged off her cloak. In an act that confused me she took two paces forward and, with an outstretched arm, gestured for me to take the discarded gown. At first I did not move, but as she made no alternate motion I grasped it with my free hand – it was coarse, damp, chilled and of a substantial weight, all at once. The girl, head still bowed, walked past me without a glance. I heard the bed in the corner creak. The stranger coughed again, this time with more ferocity; once more it was followed by a spitting noise.

The authoritative figure in the doorway, whom I knew all too well, spoke again. "Put it on," she ushered to me, "we must leave."

Tom let the information infiltrate through the layers of the minds of his readers with an expectant look on his face. It was John who spoke first: "Are you seriously suggesting that Lady Jane Grey wasn't executed after all?"

"Yes and no," said Tom, looking smug. "I mean yes that's what happened, but no, it's not me suggesting it – it's all there in black and white in her own diary. If this journal is genuine, and dating suggests that it is, it elevates Jane Grey, the sixteen-year-old niece of good King Henry VIII, right up there to one of the great British historical events that never happened.

"Carry on reading, John, and finally your question will be answered as to how these papers ended up in your house."

Chapter Nineteen

Life After Death

Aware that I was being dismissed with a second chance at life, words failed me.

13 February 1554

According to an eye witness, Guildford's carcass was thrown onto a cart and his head was brought to the chapel in a cloth. The account also said that I saw him before his death and watched as his body was returned, a warning of my own impending death.

However, I didn't see Guildford that day, alive or dead. I was over one hundred miles from London on 12 February, when he was taken from Beauchamp Tower at 10 o'clock in the morning and led to the execution area on Tower Hill. They tell me he died with great courage and dignity. I care not, for I had only bad feeling for him and what he and his family brutally took from me. Although now perhaps part of me wonders if he too had been a victim.

Feckenham's attempts in those last hours to convert me to Catholicism had delayed the executions until Monday 12 February. I had arranged my dress, composed my words and appointed the two members of my household who would accompany me and deal with me after the act had been completed. I sent the letters to my sister, Catherine, and my father who had been brought to the Tower on 10 February. I remonstrated that his actions had hastened my death. I did not write to my mother, nor did she attempt to visit me or indeed her husband. I had heard that Guildford asked to see me before he died and that Mary had granted his request. Whether this was true or not I do not know, but whatever the circumstance, I would have refused to see him.

If it wasn't for the turn of events that had occurred the previous night it would be my turn to face God, my maker.

They tell me that she wore the same black outfit I had worn at the trial. She carried my prayer book in her hands and was escorted by Sir John Brydges, the lieutenant of the Tower. My nurse, Mrs Ellen and her attendant, Mrs Tylney, also accompanied her. They both cried, but I hear the girl was calm and composed. I had watched her scaffold being erected near the White Tower, my rooms providing far too good a view of its construction. Thankfully Mary afforded me a private execution given my royal blood, and only a minimal crowd was in attendance. In this way, the girl who sacrificed her soul for me was granted some dignity and the secret was more likely to hold fast.

At the steps of the scaffold, she used the words I gave her to greet Feckenham: "God grant you all your desires and accept my own hearty thanks for all your attention to me. Although indeed, those attentions have tried me more than death can now terrify me."

I have been given a written account of exactly what had occurred, after some insistence, as my heart and soul are in torment. Let God be my witness that none of this is of my making or desire. I can only believe that it is God's will that it be like this, and I am accepting that it be of His will which is why I am not protesting the position in which I find myself.

The girl then ascended the steps and addressed the crowd, admitting that she had committed treason when she accepted the crown. I presume these words were instructed from Queen Mary, but felt true to my own. "I do wash my hands in innocency, before God and the face of you, good Christian people this day." She, I, had done no wrong. My only crime being that I was used by my feckless parents and the treacherous Dudley to further their own means. She wrung her hands and asked that those in front of her witness her death, and affirm that she died a good Christian.

She ended with yet another indication of her strong faith, for I hear she too was a good Protestant, as she said, "And now, good people, while I am alive, I pray you to assist me with your prayers." Kneeling, she asked of Feckenham, "Shall I say this psalm?" She read the 51st psalm in English and he followed her in Latin. After the prayer, she told Feckenham, "God, I beseech Him abundantly reward you for your kindness to me."

Rising to her feet, she completed her final duties. Like a princess, she handed her gloves and handkerchief to her attendant, Mrs Tylney, and her prayer-book to the lieutenant's brother, Thomas Brydges. She then began to untie her cloak and, as was the tradition, the executioner stepped forward. It was custom that the victim's outer garments became the executioner's property, but she did not know this – how could she have known this unless someone had told her? So she stepped back and desired him to leave her alone, her attendants completing the unlacing for her.

They then gave her a handkerchief to tie over her eyes. Next, the executioner knelt before her and begged her forgiveness. This, too, was a rite and one she had expected to receive. She gave her forgiveness most willingly.

She coughed and then coughed again with a little wretch, so that Mrs Tylney held a handkerchief to her mouth and some blood was removed. She appeared tired, a feeling I understand from which she had suffered for a number of months that had come with the fever and light of head. Now there was nothing to do but end it all.

The executioner asked her to stand upon the straw. Perhaps she saw the actual block for the first time as her composure faltered for just a brief moment. She whispered, "I pray you despatch me quickly," and began to kneel. She hesitated and asked, "Will you take it off before I lay me down?" referring to the blindfold. The executioner replied, "No, madam," and so she tied the handkerchief around her eyes.

I am told that when she knelt she could not find the block due to the blindfold, her arms flailed in panic for several moments as she cried out, "What shall I do? Where is it?" Those standing on the scaffold were hesitant, not knowing if they should offer assistance. I learned that finally a young man of the crowd climbed the scaffold to help her. He guided her hands to the block and hesitated as he looked at her face.

Composed now, she lowered her head and body, stretching forward to elongate her neck; her last words were, "Lord into thy hands I commend my spirit". Thankfully the executioner swung his axe and severed her head in one clean blow. Blood splattered across the scaffold and onto the onlookers said the witness. As was the nature of his duties, the executioner then briefly and quickly lifted her head and said, "So perish all the Queen's enemies. Behold, the head of a traitor." That was the end of 'Lady Jane Grey'.

I am concerned that the girl's body lay exposed and unattended for nearly four hours, spread obscenely across the blood-soaked straw. They tell me the French ambassador reported seeing it there a number of hours after the execution. Feckenham was forced to go to court for permission to be granted for her burial at St Peter-ad-Vincula since the church had recently returned to Catholicism again. Her attendants kept watch, though they were not allowed to cover the corpse, so it lay there for any bystander to see. Finally, Feckenham returned and the body was laid to rest between the bodies of two other headless queens: Anne Boleyn and Catherine Howard.

As the light began to fail I knelt and recited the Psalm 51 in memory of this poor young girl, now with God and free from her suffering.

Have mercy upon me, O God, after Thy great goodness According to the multitude of Thy mercies do away mine offenses. Wash me thoroughly from my wickedness: and cleanse me from my sin. For I acknowledge my faults: and my sin is ever before me. Against Thee only have I sinned, and done this evil in thy sight: that Thou mightiest be justified in Thy saying, and clear when Thou art judged. Behold, I was shapen in wickedness: and in sin hath my mother conceived me. But lo, thou requirest truth in the inward parts: and shalt make me to understand wisdom secretly. Thou shalt purge me with hyssop, and I shall be clean: Thou shalt wash me, and I shall be whiter than snow. Thou shalt make me hear of joy and gladness: that the bones which Thou hast broken may rejoice. Turn Thy face from my sins: and put out all my misdeeds. Make me a clean heart, O God: and renew a right spirit within me. Cast me not away from Thy presence: and take not Thy Holy Spirit from me. O give me the comfort of Thy help again: and stablish me with Thy free Spirit.

Then shall I teach Thy ways unto the wicked: and sinners shall be converted unto Thee. Deliver me from blood-guiltiness, O God, Thou that art the God of my health: and my tongue shall sing of Thy righteousness. Thou shalt open my lips, O Lord: and my mouth shall shew Thy praise. For Thou desirest no sacrifice, else would I give it Thee: but Thou delightest not in burnt-offerings. The sacrifice of God is a troubled spirit: a broken and contrite heart, O God, shalt Thou not despise. O be favourable and gracious unto Sion: build Thou the walls of Jerusalem. Then shalt Thou be pleased with the sacrifice of righteousness, with the burnt-offerings and oblations: then shall they offer young calves upon Thine altar.

It is with mixed feelings therefore that I become accustomed to my new surroundings, still reeling from the events of the past 48 hours.

After Mary had freed me from my prison, she said precious little on the long walk down the Tower and out of the fortress that was once my kingdom and then my jail. It wasn't my place to ask any questions, although many danced across my lips. When we reached a waiting carriage, Mary turned to me and placed her hands on my shoulders.

"Dear Jane," she said, "I know you are innocent and therefore I have no wish to see you die over the actions of others. Please understand though, that I cannot be seen to let you live and be further used as a pawn to forever undermine my reign. The solution I have found is the best one available – your life, along with my conscience, is spared while the country is quieted from future rebellions. The farm girl is near death anyway; her family have been rewarded handsomely for their sacrifice and she is honoured to be of service to queen and country.

"You will go to her village where you will be provided with a cottage and a dowry. You must keep your past a secret, maintain a low profile and keep to yourself. For as long as you uphold your side of the bargain, you will be allowed to live. Should you draw any attention to your situation, try to preach your Protestant ways or rouse a rebellion, then my hand will be forced and I shall not be so lenient again."

Aware that I was being dismissed with a second chance at life, words failed me. The embrace I gave Queen Mary was quite inappropriate, but the only way I knew to express my gratitude. And then, in the middle of the night, I journeyed to Cawston, which is where I find myself now. Arriving in darkness without any possessions, I found the bed by candle light, said my prayers and retired so that I could start my new life afresh in the morning.

1 March 1554

The cottage where I am staying is pleasant enough. Of course it is much smaller than Bradgate or any of my other residences, but it is well-appointed and suffices for my humbler lifestyle. There is a good fire in the main room with a table and benches, a generous kitchen with a pantry and store rooms, a study filled with natural light where I have a writing desk and chair, and two bedrooms with canopy beds, wardrobes and dressers.

I have upheld the requirements of my release and kept to myself in the weeks that I have been resident here in

Cawston, going out only to buy provisions. The dreary weather has enabled me to attend the market for supplies with my cloak pulled tightly around me and the hood hanging low over my face. No one stops me and I am able to go about my business without interruption. However, I am plagued by visits from Mr Sawer from the church, who seems insistent to make my acquaintance. I have been as curt as I can to dissuade him, but still he finds reasons to call on me: might I join the church service, have I seen the wares available in the market, do I need any assistance with the house since the heavy rains? It is not in my nature to be so awful to such a kind man, but I must respect the conditions of my release and so have kept my responses curt.

21 March 1554

The bleak clutches of winter are finally lifting and the buds of spring are emerging to give the countryside canvas an air of hope. This reflects my mood. Since being freed from the Tower prison where I had a sociable life, I have barely spoken to a soul, except for to discourage Mr Sawer. However, the sunshine heralds a new dawn and I am determined to put my confinement to benefit, otherwise why was I spared?

Abiding by cousin Mary's conditions, I will not converse with anyone directly, but I have assumed an anonymous identity to start a few correspondence relationships. I have contacted John Aylmer and Roger Ascham under my new guise, saying that the late Lady Jane Grey had recommended their services and asking if they could assist me with my studies from a distance. This way I will keep active of mind and make the most of my second chance.

The change in weather has also afforded me the opportunity to tend to the garden that accompanies the cottage. On one of my many walks around the village I noticed Mr Sawer's manor had the most magnificent floral displays and so I sought his advice on which flowers would work well in the clay soil I find here, and which fruit and vegetables I might be able to cultivate for personal use. I have never tried my hand at gardening before and find this new hobby very restorative. Here Mr Sawer and I find comfortable conversation and I am able to have some human contact without discussing anything personal. Although he has tenant farmers and does not farm the land himself, he is knowledgeable in the theory and delighted to instruct me in the best practices.

21 June 1554

It has been several months since I moved to Cawston and I am pleased to have found a natural flow to my routine. Much of my time is spent tending to the garden were I grow most of my own food. Although I don't need to buy much, I still visit the marketplace regularly to feel among the people, but of course I am careful not to engage anyone in conversation. I receive the same succour from attending church every Sunday, although I always sit at the back on a pew alone. Sometimes I wonder what the rest of the congregation think of me, but I have an inner peace which helps me past such trivial concerns. I use the rest of my time to converse with my tutors on spiritual matters, in a variety of languages, and find it most stimulating to stretch my ability in this way.

The only person I speak to is Mr. Sawer. Having sought his advice on the garden, he drops by regularly to monitor his student's progress and offer his wisdom whenever he spies a problem. I began to offer him some refreshment in return for his help and our discussions diversified beyond horticulture. He is the churchwarden, so naturally we discuss religion and I was delighted to learn that he too was Protestant. The parish church remains that way presently, but I fear that Queen Mary's fervent Catholicism will demand changes before the year is out. She is making a terrible name for herself persecuting prominent Protestants, but I am mindful to avoid any commentary on my cousin and fail to respond whenever Mr. Sawer makes reference to any members of the royal family.

2 November 1556

Mr. Sawer came round today as normal. Rather than our usual discourse on matters of theology or religion, he was verbose about the harvest which has failed for the second year in a row. Cawston has witnessed many winter deaths following such poor yields and he fears for a number of the parish. His concern is admirable, but then I do not know the residents here in the same way he does. Although I have lived among their bosom for two and a half years, I have kept my distance in order to fulfil my promise to cousin Mary.

When I ask Mr. Sawer what he intends to do to help the wretched and poor, he shrugs his shoulders and asks in reply, "What can I do?" Torn that my precious relationship with Mr. Sawer urges me not to antagonise him, I struggle to hold my tongue as I know that he will benefit from increased prices for the food produced on his land. In addition, the wool from his sheep is selling well, so while he says he has sympathy for the poor, he is not personally affected. Although he is a good man for his concern, I can't help but feel that there is more to be done.

19 December 1556

Christmas is nearly upon us and it is a time of goodwill to all men. It is with this in mind that I have opened my house to some of the poor of the village. My garden still thrives and I cook up a vast broth every lunchtime. Those that have no food can come and enjoy a warming cup of soup in front of a roaring fire before returning to their search for work. I do not charge any money and am rewarded solely by the comfort of my benevolence. Mr. Sawer is not happy that I offer such charity, but has no rights to stop me. I will continue for as long as the poor of Cawston need me.

30 June 1557

Sad news has reached me that England has joined Spain in war against France. This is clearly the result of cousin Mary's Catholic allegiance to the Holy Roman Emperor and the influence of her husband, for I don't think that anyone in this great land wishes to fight our old enemy again. I fear that the queen's popularity, once so strong as to depose my claim to the throne, has dwindled as a direct result of the actions she has taken both at home and abroad in the name of her religion. The men of the village are reluctant to fight and I fear they may riot if forced.

15 December 1558

I am told that cousin Mary was weak and ill from May, and she thankfully was relieved of her suffering in the morning of 17 November 1558 at the Palace of St. James. That would make forty and two years. There was an influenza outbreak that had spread to the regions and killed many. This epidemic also claimed the life of

Reginald Pole the Catholic Cardinal later the same day. I was told that my blessed queen was in much pain at the end and I prayed for her soul. She wished to be buried next to her mother, Catherine, at the Abbey in Peterborough, but is to be interred in the Abbey at Westminster.

During the service which took place yesterday, the Bishop of Westminster, John White, praised Queen Mary, stating: "She was a King's daughter; she was a King's sister; she was a King's wife. She was a Queen, and by the same title a king also."

To me she was my queen, but also my cousin who, in her deed, risked everything for the sake of my life. Whether it was right that I should have been spared in this way, God will decide. Whether my life spared has been a good one I cannot say; my guilt overcomes me to admit that sometimes I think it would have easier if I had been taken into the hands of my God on that cold February morning.

But that was not the wish of Queen Mary and I have always been an obedient servant, first to my God and then to the Crown. I hope I have made amends these past few years for any wrongdoing. For as long as I breathe, I will strive to be a better person in Mary's name.

What life holds for me now, I am unsure. Elizabeth will ascend to the crown, but I know not whether she is aware of my presence.

20 December 1565

This winter has been particularly harsh which seems bitterly unfair after such a weak harvest. The poor just don't have enough food to survive and I have heard of many deaths in the village already. Again this year I have chosen to operate the open house lunches that I produced in previous bad years. The poor are exceptionally grateful, but Mr. Sawer warned me that it was not popular with the hard-working honest folk of the towne. They do not feel that the unemployed should be helped with food handouts.

29 December 1565

Choking awake one morning after Christmas, I discovered my bedroom was thick with black smoke. Fear disoriented me and I failed to locate the door to the stairs. I cried out for help, but realised that I lived in such a remote location my calls would go unanswered. Besides, taking a deep breath to shout only made me cough more.

Covering my nose and mouth with my left hand, I used the other to help navigate around the room to find the entrance. Heaving the door open, I was blasted by a wall of heat and smoke thicker than before. I could not see any flames, but heard the roar and crackle of a fire. I made my way down the stairs and discovered the kitchen of my cottage ablaze. I anticipated that this would be the way I would expire, but did not fear death itself. I had faced it once before and made my peace. If He chose to take me, then I would go willingly, however I wanted to preserve the changes I have made since last He spared me. Being raised by materialistic parents has left me cold to possessions and since coming to Cawston I have nothing of value except for my journal.

Overcome with fumes, I ran to my writing desk and gathered up my personal notes, letters and studies, as much as I could carry. The destructive forces were fast taking hold of my residence and my path to the front door was blocked with fallen timber. Climbing over the obstacles, clutching my papers to my chest, I reached the door and flung it open, desperate for fresh air. Opening my escape route only served to fan the flames which licked at my feet at the influx of air. Never before have I felt such searing pain. Unable to stand, all I could think to do was drag myself out to the grass and roll around.

Thankfully my dress did not catch fire, but my legs were badly burned and blistered. I crawled as far as I could and lay on my books protectively. It was there that Mr. Sawer found me, passed out from pain and smoke inhalation. He brought me and my belongings to his servant's house for recuperation, and it from these quarters, a day later, that I write this entry.

31 December 1565

Two days have passed since Mr Sawer saved me from certain death, but I am not sure that is His will. My injuries are severe and debilitating. My breathing is shallow as my lungs still feel raw from the smoke and I frequently cough blood. My legs are deformed and look like molten wax. The blister wounds on my feet will not heal and I am unable to walk. It may be that if He spares me once more, I am left a cripple. My cottage anyway is already a ghost of the past.

Mr Sawer keeps asking me how the fire came about. I cannot say if it was deliberate, or just an unfortunate accident. Mr Sawer seems to suggest that it was God's retribution for my unlawful help to the poor. We have a different God, Mr Sawer and I.

The medicine man visits me regularly, but cannot offer anything to cure my ailments. I see him in earnest discussion with Mr Sawer, but neither will tell me the outcome of their conversation. A visit from the parish priest this morning speaks volumes of my prognosis. He prayed with me for a long time, but I was not up to our usual religious debate. I fear I won't see the New Year and so this will be my last entry until I am well again. I will hide this journal to protect cousin Mary's most precious secret.

John shook his head when he had finished reading. "Well I never," he said slowly. "So Lady Jane Grey died in the servant's house of Sawer's manor, which is what we've just renovated?"

"It would appear that way," agreed Tom. "There are no further entries in the journal, so we can only deduce that the hole from which Alice retrieved the book, was the safe place Jane found to hide her journal and Queen Mary's secret."

"When was she born?" asked Alice.

"1537," replied John and Tom in unison.

"Wow, she wasn't even 30 years old – what an eventful life. So what happens now? I mean this discovery literally changes history books forever, doesn't it?"

"Well, yes," replied Tom. "But before we discuss that, there's more. There were a few loose leaf pages which were virtually untouched and are just as revealing."

Chapter Twenty

Mary's Last Act

My reign has been one of turmoil, strife and difficulty and I have not been happy. However, I am content that I did the right thing.

"Let me ask you a question," posed Tom tantalisingly, his lips twitching with excitement. "Have you ever seen a picture, a painting or a verified image of Lady Jane Grey? And before you say, 'The one of her in a satin white dress in a darkened room, wearing a blindfold with her hand outstretched seeking the block before her execution' – it was painted much later by Paul Delaroche and has no historical accuracy or relevance. Eye witness accounts state she wore a black dress, so it's nothing more than just a pretty, or macabre, picture that has sometimes been used to sexualise the brutal death of a young lady."

He left a dramatic pause before resolving his own query: "The short answer is no: no picture exists of Lady Jane Grey. There is said to be a likeness hanging in the National Portrait Gallery, but there is no proof that the painting is actually of her, and in fact it has been derided by historians such as Dr David Starkey who, momentarily branching out from Henry VIII, stated: 'It's an appallingly bad picture and there's absolutely no reason to suppose it's got anything to do with Lady Jane Grey. There is no documentary evidence, no evidence from inventories, jewellery or heraldry to support the idea this is Lady Jane Grey.'

"So, my next question is this: don't you think it's odd that a one-time queen of England, even if only for nine days, has no pictorial record? Not one? Particularly at a time when court artists were knocking them out at a fair old rate to make a crust. Well… now we know why!"

Tom's triumph was met with a pregnant pause as the trio in front of him looked bemused. He reached in his bag and pulled out an A3-sized piece of paper which contained a photocopy of three other pages. "Here we are," he said, handing it to Alice. She was silent for a while as she scanned the text. "They've done a great job of enhancing the script," she said, "there's no way I could have made anything out when we first found it."

Elliot looked over Alice's shoulder, but was none the wiser as the whole thing was still in the original sixteenth-century Latin. Alice, meanwhile, was busily translating it in her head, but clearly getting some of it wrong as she concluded that it didn't make much sense: "I don't get it – why was Jane considered a traitor for looking in the mirror?"

Tom handed a similar-looking piece of paper to John. "I'm glad you didn't give that to me," commented Elliot, "as I was off school the day we did Latin."

"Don't worry, I can't read Latin either – this is the translated version for the uneducated among us. John, perhaps you'd like to read it out so we're all on the same page?" Five minutes later, when John had finished reading Lady Jane Grey's account of Mary's public announcement, they all sat in stunned silence.

"That was my reaction too," said Tom.

"So, let me get this right," said Alice, "Queen Mary – Mary I, Bloody Mary, or whatever else you want to call her – ordered that all pictures of Lady Jane Grey be destroyed on the day of her execution? Then she announced that anyone found with an image of her, or purporting to be her, would be charged with treason against the crown and end up in the same predicament as Jane? She wanted every single reference to Jane erased, just like her existence on this earth?"

"That's true", agreed Tom, "although obviously there would remain accounts of her life up to that time, of her nine-day claim to fame and the execution itself. Mary couldn't literally eradicate her cousin from history books altogether, but without any portraits, her likeness would quickly fade in people's memory and her importance would be diminished. It paints Mary in an even worse light than the one history already tells us."

"Is that it then?" asked Alice. "Bloody Mary was not only a reactionary religious fanatic who ordered all Protestant heretics be burnt, but she was also a paranoid bitch who wanted to expunge her cousin's image from history?"

"Never liked her - old frump" added Elliot, "much preferred her sister, Elizabeth. All that lime dusted face and blackened teeth – you know, a real looker."

"Well, yes, those are the conclusions that everyone has reached until now," corrected Tom. "It would appear that she had a heart after all. The journal entries I showed you before jumped from 1558 to her death in 1565. Information on the intervening years was found on some of the loose leaf pages we found and I think Jane was as surprised by the turn of events as you will be when you read them."

Before handing out the translations of the final few pages, Tom set the context. Queen Mary I had died on the morning of 17 November 1558 and was succeeded by her half-sister Elizabeth. Once Edward had been born in 1537, few in the royal palace would have believed that his older half-sister, Mary, let alone Elizabeth, would have ever succeeded the throne. Elizabeth was considered by most as equally illegitimate as Mary, because Henry shouldn't have been allowed to divorce his first wife, Catherine, or marry his second wife, Anne.

Like Lady Jane Grey, Princess Elizabeth was accused of being involved in the failed Wyatt's rebellion against Queen Mary in 1554 and the presence of a Protestant heir with a legitimate claim to the throne remained a constant and real threat. As we now know, both potential traitors were spared execution, but while Lady Jane Grey's reprise was kept secret, Princess Elizabeth was interred under house arrest at the gatehouse of Woodstock Manor.

Like Jane, Elizabeth was well-educated, apparently fluent in six languages, and had inherited intelligence, determination and shrewdness from both her parents. Records tell us that Elizabeth was much more of a consensus queen when she occupied the throne than Mary ever was, or indeed her father, Henry. During Elizabeth's reign, the Church of England was secured and its doctrines were established in thirty-nine articles of 1563, which was a successful compromise between Roman Catholicism and Protestantism, largely appeasing both parties and seemingly popular with the nation.

Elizabeth inherited a number of problems stirred up by Mary's reign when she took to the throne in 1558. The country was at war with France, which put a tremendous strain on the royal coffers and increased tensions between the religious factions. Astute and swift to act, Queen Elizabeth addressed these pressing issues during the first session of Parliament in 1559. She called for the passage of the Act of Supremacy, which re-established the Church of England with a common prayer book and enabled the adoption of a moderate approach to the divisive conflict between Puritans and Catholics. Elizabeth said there was only one Jesus Christ, and that the rest was simply a dispute over details.

Fending off attempts to remove her from the throne was another hurdle for the young queen, and by far the greatest risk was posed by her cousin the Catholic Mary Stuart, Queen of Scots, the daughter of King James V of Scotland. Mary had briefly united Scotland and France when she married King Francis II in 1558, and continued to threaten Elizabeth's reign when she returned to Scotland in 1561 after Francis' death. Many Catholics believed Mary to be the rightful heir to the throne of England and numerous plots were hatched to depose Elizabeth in favour of Mary. When Mary Stuart herself was implicated in such schemes, Elizabeth responded by jailing her in 1567.

Like Queen Mary I's treatment of Lady Jane Grey, Elizabeth was reluctant to sign a death warrant for her cousin, although it was reported that she disliked her intensely but instead imprisoned Mary for twenty years before finally agreeing to have her executed in 1587. Perhaps her procrastination was due, in some small part, to a letter Elizabeth received from the late Queen Mary. It had been entrusted to her most faithful servant on her deathbed and was delivered with the red wax seal still intact, to be read by Queen Elizabeth alone. Tom explained that the letter was found among the loose leaf pages of Jane's journal and he handed out translations of both documents.

11 November 1558

My sister Elizabeth,

When you read this letter, my duty will be done and you will be queen. My fear was that this letter should fall into the wrong hands, and the secrets it bears may be used against me. But now I am gone, it is of no consequence for history can be blamed.

You, like the rest of the nation, believe that our cousin Jane was executed on 12 February, of the year 1554. However, I believed, as did many others around me, that Jane was a child who had little, or nothing, to do with the plot against me to put her on the throne. Only a fool would not know that it was the actions of her father, Henry Grey, Duke of Suffolk, and John Dudley, Duke of Northumberland.

I am also clear that when our brother lay on his death bed and nominated Jane as his successor, thus subverting the claims of both yourself and I under the Third Succession Act, he also had little to do with this decision. When the Privy Council changed sides, placing me as queen on July 19, there was no option but to attribute charges of high treason and then carry out the sentence for such an act.

I was hoping that Jane's life could be spared by converting her faith, but Jane, being Jane, would not convert to Catholicism; she was honourable to her faith to the end. However, I could not and did not wish to see this course of action taken and when an opportunity fell into my lap to change this, I took it. I trust that you will understand the decision I made for our cousin Jane.

No one has suspected anything. Indeed, the mere suggestion that I had sent Jane to the country would be preposterous. I can tell you now though, that Jane was not executed on 12 February, but an ill farmworker's daughter took her place instead. The girl bore such a resemblance to Jane that you could not tell them apart, even when next to each other the day before one of them died.

I attended the Tower where Jane was imprisoned the night before the execution and oversaw the change myself. I alone took the girl to take Jane's place. This poor wretch was at the time ill and dying of consumption and coughing blood. This peasant's daughter would possibly have died within days or perhaps weeks anyway and I ensured that the family would be sufficiently compensated for their loss. I ordered the destruction of all pictures of Jane so that there could be no question of the deception and now only memories can tell us what Jane looked like.

I tell you all this in the hope that you will do two things: first to ensure Jane's continued safety, maintain her grant and remind her of the conditions of her release; second, to record Jane's portrait so that her image is not completely lost to history. I had them all destroyed so that Jane would be safe from the risk of her being recognised.

Jane will not be expecting you or any visitors, she is virtually a recluse bar one gentleman caller from the village who only knows her as an educated lonely widow. I visited her once within the last year when I thought I was pregnant, but have not returned since. Now I know I will not produce an heir, I beseech you as my successor to carry out my wishes for our cousin.

My reign has been one of turmoil, strife and difficulty and I have not been happy. However, I am content that I did the right thing by cousin Jane. Whether Jane is happy, I cannot say. I hope dear sister that you can allow her to continue the life that she has been living under my name. God save my soul.

May you, your Most Christian Majesty, accept this not as a burden, for my conscience is now relieved.

Yours, Mary.

5 April 1559

The days are just beginning to grow longer and the nights warmer, thank goodness. Dusk was approaching today when I heard the unmistakable sound of horseshoes on the lane fast approaching the house. At this time of year, I have no visitors other than Mr. Sawer, and he calls in the morning and does not come by horse. Occasionally a lost and weary traveller might come my way by mistake, looking for directions, food or shelter, but being a lone woman of some financial means I was always wary of being robbed and so refused them entry.

In the years I have been trapped here in Cawston, I have only received one genuine caller on horseback, and that was cousin Mary last year when she thought she might bear a child. I was not prepared for such an appearance and did not know what to say to someone who was both my saviour and captor. I trusted God to look after me during the meeting and it passed without incidence. But my dear queen has since passed and so it was with trepidation that I braced myself at the sound of hooves advancing toward my door.

Peering out of the window I gauged that they looked to be good horses, not the type favoured by travellers or market traders, so I deduced these people were here on business; the Queen's business I feared.

Running away was not an option, for if they were here on business, they would surely come back until they found me. Likewise, failing to find me if I hid in the false room built for just such a circumstance would only encourage them to return again. So I decided to open the door and accept with good grace the new consequences my position brought me. When the two visitors dismounted, I saw one was female and one was male; the female had a hood which partly obscured her face.

"You're a long way from the road, can I help you?" I enquired, in the lightest tone I could muster.

The man spoke first: "We have a message for you from the Queen of England."

"A message from the queen, from Queen Elizabeth, the new queen?" I clarified, wracking my brain as to how she would know of my existence. "Then you had best come in," I said gesturing for my guests to enter the cottage. "What business would the queen have with me?" I asked as innocently as possible.

The lady removed her hood to reveal a flock of auburn hair and I recognised her immediately as my cousin, Elizabeth. I dropped into a deep curtsey: "Your Majesty."

"Jane," whispered Elizabeth as she took my hand and motioned for me to stand. I froze at the use of my name as I had not heard my moniker spoken for a good while. "Jane, dearest cousin Jane, you have been so wronged. Like me, you have escaped death, but you have been confined to a life of secrecy, while I have been free to speak my mind and live as I choose. I received this letter from Mary and thought you should have it for safe keeping."

Taking the letter from cousin Elizabeth, I noted that my hands were shaking. The evening that I previously thought mild, suddenly left me chilled to the bone. There was silence as I failed to respond.

Elizabeth answered my unasked question of what would happen next. "I could invite you back to my court, for who would suspect that it could be you, but I fear any risk is too great to take such a chance. I can't be sure that no one would notice or find out what happened, and so my hands are tied. I can only continue to provide you with a grant and protect you as long as you stay here in Cawston. You will remain as you are now, a widowed lady of the village who people know very little about, a lady who keeps to herself. I am sorry, but I can offer no more.

"There is one more thing, something which Mary asked me to do. After your execution, every picture of you was destroyed to prevent your new identity being discovered, so there are no paintings of you anywhere in court, at Bradgate House, or throughout the Kingdom; the only recollection anybody has of your face is in their heads. Mary wanted this to be rectified.

"I have arranged for the court artist, Levina Teerlinc, to come here to paint your likeness. This commission will never go on public display or be seen by anybody else, but it will remain with me as a record of your existence. I shall have it as a memory of how my dear cousin Jane looked."

Still not knowing what to say, I stared down at the letter and read the words of regret from Mary. Elizabeth then asked me a strange question, "Are you happy, Jane?"

"Happy? I don't know really how to apply the word happy to my circumstances," I replied, as honestly as I could. "I'm happy that I am able to wake up each morning and witness the wonderful world that God has created and given us; the sunshine, the rain, flora and fauna, the sound of birds singing. That makes me happy." Unsure of what to say next, I paused. Elizabeth nodded approval for me to continue.

"I am lonely, Your Majesty. I cannot live a normal life and must hide myself in the shadows. But I am not ungrateful and I have devoted my life to the studies of God and of caring for my fellow man in His name. All of my actions are dictated by God, so as long as it is His will for me to still be here on this earth, then I am blessed. God will decide when it is time for me to be taken, until then I will use my time to the best of my ability."

It was my cousin's turn to remain silent, clearly thinking upon my comments. "You'll not see me again and you'll receive no more visitors from the court. I will establish a line of communication to me, but it should only be used in the case of an extreme emergency or distress. I clearly cannot have you back at court, or reviving your life as Lady Jane Grey, but as a fellow Protestant I feel less threat from you, not least with increasing years of your perceived passing, than my sister Mary would have felt.

"Perchance you could go about your business with a bit more freedom, mayhap strike up conversation in the market place, or cultivate a friendship or two. This is still all to be under your assumed identity and under no circumstance may you divulge your past. Be warned though that this privilege can be reversed, as can Mary's leniency, should I hear of any rebellion or uprising in your name."

"You are most gracious, Your Majesty," I said as I curtseyed and wiped a stray tear from my cheek. "I will not let you down."

"I hope this brings you some solace. You are in my heart, Jane." Elizabeth took both my hands in hers. "Take care, cousin Jane, take care." Pulling her hood back over her distinctive hair, she turned and walked out the door.

10 April 1559

A few days have passed since I spoke with cousin Elizabeth and, true to her word, today I received a visit from Levina Teerlinc. She will stay with me at the keeper's cottage for a period of nearly six weeks. That in itself is a gift; manna from heaven to have somebody other than Mr. Sawer with whom I could converse meaningfully.

Levina is somewhat older than me and quite an astonishing woman. At dinner tonight I insisted to learn more about my guest and she divulged a most fascinating life. I shall record our conversation here as accurately as I can remember:

"I was born into a South Netherlandish family of illuminators, my grandfather was Alexander Bening and my father was Simon Benning. As the eldest of five girls and in lieu of a son and heir, my father instructed me in his trade; the Ghent-Bruges school of manuscript illumination. With hand-written and illustrated books losing out to printed text, my father turned his hand to portrait miniatures for his wealthier patrons. The locket-sized likenesses proved very popular as a keepsake of a loved one, or a way of introducing two people proposed in marriage who live some distance apart.

"I worked with my father in his workshop for several years, finessing my art, and during that time I was introduced to George Teerlinc. We were married quickly and continued to live in Bruges, until I received an invitation from Catherine Parr. Apparently she was familiar with my work and, in 1546 when she was still queen, she summoned me to the English court. The previous limner, Lucas Horenbout, had passed two years earlier and she thought I might take the position. Of course, King Henry VIII was less open-minded about the idea of a woman holding such a post, but once he saw my work I was honoured to be officially appointed in November. I'm told that my starting annuity of 40 pounds was an increase on the previous income for this role."

"That is high praise indeed," I commented, "and something of which you should be proud. Catherine was a very astute woman, I am not surprised she noticed and promoted your talent."

"Did you have the privilege of knowing the queen?"

Not wanting to give too much away I suggested I had merely met her in passing. "It is widely acknowledged that she was always very fair, and of course she was particularly passionate about educating young ladies."

"Indeed, that is true," Levina continued, unaware of my racing heart. "A few years later, after Henry had died, Catherine invited Lady Elizabeth Tudor and the young Lady Jane Grey to stay in her household at Sudeley Castle. The residence acquired a good reputation for being a respected place of learning for young women. It was such a shame to think of the scandal of Sir Thomas and Lady Elizabeth, and then of Catherine's passing after childbirth."

It was alarming to hear of my own childhood experiences spoken in such a candid way, while I was unable to even utter my own name or see my image in a reflection. I moved the conversation forward as I did not want to dwell on such a sad time in my life. "So, other than your royal appointment, tell me who else you have worked with?"

"Many families also present in the court: namely the Dudleys, Seymours and Greys." She studied my face intently for a while, which I took simply to be part of her work until she said, "Actually, I did a portrait of Catherine Grey and it is remarkable how much like her you look."

Trying hard not to let my reactions give me away, I discreetly enquired about my mother and my sisters, generally asking after their well-being since the demise of the man of the house and the eldest daughter (that is to say, my father and me). "The Duchess, Lady Catherine and Lady Mary settled back in court after the terrible deaths of Henry and Jane Grey and retained Queen Mary's favour during her reign. Frances Grey remarried the year after her husband was executed and sadly had three unsuccessful attempts to have more children. Her two surviving daughters are now fostering good relations with the new queen as they have become the heirs presumptive if Elizabeth remains childless.

"John Dudley's son, Robert, has gone to great lengths to regain royal favour since his family's disgrace and he too is now a close friend of Queen Elizabeth, having recently been appointed to Master of the Horse. Likewise, Edward Seymour's son, Edward, has also worked hard to restore the good name of his family and Elizabeth has reinstated his peerage, creating for him the 1st Earl of Hertford. Life moves on and yet stays the same."

18 April 1559

Levina Teerlinc has been outlining my form this last week in charcoal and has today started filling in my portrait. I have asked several times if I may see the work in progress, but she firmly rebuffs me, reminding me of the virtue of patience. Having discussed her background at the start of the week, the conversation has moved on to the process of her artistry.

"A big portrait like this is unusual for me as I normally work in miniatures," she explained as we broke for lunch. "They are used mostly for diplomatic purposes or gifts. I enjoy the challenge of working on such a small scale. I know that it is for many people painstaking and fiddly work, but I relish the precision of such minute detail. For this type of work, I use oil-based paints, but for the miniatures I use watercolour on vellum. But enough about me – pray tell me a bit about yourself, so that I may know the person I am to portray."

"Me?" I queried in surprise. No one had asked anything about me, or showed concern for my thoughts for a very long time, yet this was the second time in as many weeks that someone had asked directly about me. I did not know where to start. "What do you want to know?"

"Well, let me see: where you come from, what your childhood was like and how you came to reside here, in this village of Cawston?"

I took a deep breath and stared at the vegetables I stirred in the pot on the stove as I contemplated the answer to those fine questions. How had I come to live here, how could I explain my life so far? I had a promise to keep to my cousin, the queen, but I had come to know Levina and we had discussed so many other things that I desperately wanted to unburden my secret. I kept my gaze lowered and answered as succinctly as I could.

"I cannot say much of my formative years; my parents were very strict and I formed no real relationship with them. It was a cold and oppressive start to life, but I was fortunate enough to escape their bullying to the bosom of a lovely, kind ward named Catherine, where I was afforded warmth and affection. I was provided with a fine education from an excellent tutor and quickly became fluent in Latin, as well as the languages native to Italy, Greece and France. I had a natural talent as a linguist and thrived in such a positive environment.

"However, just a couple of years later, when I was no more than eleven years old, my dear sweet ward passed soon after childbirth. Heartbroken, I was sent back home where an acquaintance of my parents took over control of my life. I didn't know it then, but now I can see this man was a calculating and ambitious politician who manipulated our family for his own gain. He proposed my marriage to his son, to which I objected, but was ultimately forced into by my mother. My ward simultaneously persuaded the man he was advising to change his will so that I could inherit his title and riches."

I finally looked up from the food. Had Levina managed to piece together my story? She had already commented on my resemblance to Lady Catherine Grey, but had she now guessed the family name of my heritage? "The man I was forced to marry died not long after our nuptials and, as a widow, I was finally able to free myself from these ties. I escaped and ran away to this village where I have assumed a new identity." I hung my head again, acutely humiliated by how little control I had possessed over the course of my life. This was painfully apparent as I saw in front of me someone who had moulded her life the way she wanted, becoming one of the country's most respected portrait painters, and a woman besides. "Some might say my confinement here is a fate worse than death, but I let God be the judge of that. I spend much of my time here trying to amend for the wrong I have done in my life. I was but a pawn in everyone else's game, so now I strive to take charge."

It is to Levina's credit that she took my confession in her stride. I was careful to keep my story anonymous, but given that she mixed in the same circles, it would not have been beyond the realms of possibility that she could have put the elements together to uncover the truth. Whether or not she guessed my real lineage, she did not pry further and it was never mentioned again.

20 May 1559

Six weeks has slipped by in glorious companionship. I have felt a sense of joy and validation through sharing each precious day with someone that I have not felt for many years. I wish Levina could stay forever, but sadly our time together has to pass and all too soon she has finished her work. Before she wrapped the painting up for transport, she finally unveiled it to me.

If I describe it as a stunning picture, know that I do not say it vainly, but meaning that she is a gifted woman who uses her talent to bring a flat canvas to life. It bore resemblance to me, but also portrayed me in a royal fashion to which I am unaccustomed and so I could admire it easily without feeling as though I was looking in a mirror. I am honoured that cousin Elizabeth saw it fit to commission such a piece and hope she will consult it when she is required to take a tough decision, and be reminded of the brave step taken in secret by her half-sister Mary to save my soul.

Having packed her bags and secured the portrait for transit, as Levina was leaving she lent in toward me and grasped my hands in hers. She searched for words, but found none. Instead she pressed something small and hard into my palms. Eventually she whispered, "I wonder if this token of friendship can make up for any of your pain or loneliness," before turning and walking out of my life forever.

After some time I was able to prize my hands apart, and I saw she had simultaneously created a miniature of my likeness while painting the commissioned portrait. Levina had given me a true gift: something which, no matter the size, proved I existed.

Epilogue

Concluding that the journal and papers had literally rewritten history, Tom began to explain the next steps to John. As the documents were found on his property, he would be recorded as the registered owner, but clearly they were of national interest and should be surrendered to various institutions for further study. He advised that John should make the find known to the British Museum who would be able to undertake many more tests to verify the validity of the papers and testify their legitimacy. There would then be a raft of experts clamouring to trawl through the information, discuss the ramifications, make counter claims and dismiss the facts in equal measure.

"Through all of this John, you will have to consider whether or not you want any associated publicity, because once this becomes public knowledge, it will likely explode. You could be on the front cover of every national newspaper, and appear on every daytime chat show if you wanted."

"What, you mean I could be on *Richard and Judy, Feck*?" joked John, artlessly showing his age.

"If that's what you want, mate."

"Wow," said John, somewhat taken aback. "That is a lot of information to take in." He fell quiet as he contemplated his next steps, leaving Alice and Elliot to muse about the latest revelation.

Alice, who had been very involved in researching the first lot of papers now had the bit between her teeth. "So not only was Lady Jane Grey's life spared, but there also exists two portraits of our Nine Days' Queen, who Sawer knew simply as the widow of keeper's cottage, as painted by Levina Teerlinc? They must still be hidden somewhere. It would be heart-breaking to think they might have been destroyed after Mary and Elizabeth went to such great lengths to correct history. But if these papers can crawl out of the woodwork after hundreds of years, there's no reason to believe the same can't be true of the pictures." Tom hadn't heard all of Alice's monologue as she had been mumbling, talking it through to herself as much as telling her companions.

"Hey, do you guys know that there is a miniature portrait in the Victoria and Albert museum which is unaccounted for?" Alice had clearly been doing some more research in the intervening period as she shared some unexpected information. "It is of an unknown woman, showing her head and shoulders wearing a bonnet with a white fur collar and a gold necklace crucifix. It is a small piece, about 25 mm in diameter and 47 mm in height, thought to be painted around 1560. Could it be the missing token of friendship from Levina to Jane? With this new information, I bet it will be put back under the microscope to determine its origins. If only we could find the large secret portrait commissioned by Queen Elizabeth, perhaps stored in an attic or basement somewhere, then we would have some visual proof of what Lady Jane Grey looked like in her later days, living in obscurity in a Norfolk village. Then we could cross reference it to the miniature."

Tom was sceptical that either portrait had survived the centuries and was more focussed on the words that had actually been found in a journal believed to be that of Lady Jane Grey, and corroborated by the papers of George Sawer. These two sources gave credence to a new theory about the fate of Lady Jane Grey and may be backed up by other writings from the period. "We do not know how or when she eventually died, all we have is the last diary entry before she hid it," he concluded. "One thing that is clear, however, is that Queen Mary I did have a heart after all and compassion for her family. Despite the high personal risk to herself, she could not and did not see her sixteen-year-old cousin, who she knew to be innocent, go to the block.

"History should record this."

The End

AUTHOR'S NOTE

In telling this fictional version of the story of Lady Jane Grey I have adhered to the facts where they are known, documented and fit with the narrative. However, I have used dramatic licence and put names and faces to some reports and to unknown eye witness accounts; for example, the boy mentioned at 'Jane's' execution.

I have had the benefit of being able to quote from contemporary documents and letters which are determined as genuine although I have sometimes used them out of context, for example the letter Jane wrote to her sister Katherine.

The long accepted view that the parents of Jane, the Suffolk's, were harsh and unforgiving, particularly her mother, which has been recently challenged, I have stuck with. Despite a softened view of them in recent opinions there is no credible way of explaining away Jane's own bitter testimony that was recorded first hand by Roger Ascham. And at least one contemporary source records Jane being beaten and cursed when she resisted her betrothal to Guildford Dudley. Recent research by Nicola Tallis suggest that the traditional view of the Suffolk's being hard, over bearing and selfish parent is a correct one. There seems little credible evidence that there has been a deliberate attempt over the centuries to blacken Frances's name.

I consulted numerous different texts to inform my view of Tudor England to create characters that may have existed. The following works have all been used:

Lisle, Leanda de: The Sisters Who Would Be Queen (London 2008)

Plowden, Alison: Lady Jane Grey; Nine Days Queen (Stroud, 2003)

Stevenson, Joan: The Greys of Bradgate (Leicester, 1974)

Apart from these and other references I have reconstructed Jane's life from external evidence, inference and probability of events happening given the context of the time.

Sadly, the North's and the Cobham's are fictitious; William Cobham is likewise, however some of the people he meets do appears on contemporary reports for example Thomas Pole the Norwich merchant. Similarly, the harsh winters resulting in poor harvests have also been taken from reports of the time. As any attentive school boy or girl can confirm the Kett rebellion of 1549 was genuine. Robert Kett was a yeoman farmer, a native of Wymondham, Norfolk. Little is known of his early life, but we certainly know about the end of it. In 1549 Kett led a rebellion against the practice of enclosure of common land. In order to understand the rebellion and the light in which authorities saw it, you have to look at two events that created enormous social turmoil in early 16th century England; the enclosure movement and the dawn of the Reformation.

One of the traditional rights enjoyed by Kett and his social equals was the right to graze animals on common land. However, in the Tudor period local land owners (the nobility and rising merchant classes) began to enclose common land and use it to graze their own sheep, in the process removing that formerly accessible land from farming by villagers and small farmers. This enclosure allowed landowners to create great wealth by selling wool. By enclosing common land and using it to raise sheep, landowners became rich, but at the same time, peasants and yeoman farmers like Kett, who used common land for subsistence farming and raising animals, now found it hard to survive, let alone thrive. Unrest came in the form of violent events and in 1549 culminated in Kett's Rebellion.

Robert Kett was captured a few miles from the battle site. He was taken to the Tower of London, held for a time, then tried for treason. The outcome of the trial was inevitable. He was found guilty, and transported back to Norwich to be executed. He was hanged in chains from the walls of Norwich Castle, and allowed to die of starvation. His corpse was left hanging long after his death, to act as a warning to the people of Norwich of the fate that awaited traitors.

The manner in which I portrayed Queen Mary was a dilemma; Bloody Mary as she has been known doesn't leave much to the imagination. However, rather than simply take the traditional view I decided to look a little deeper into her actions and behaviour before and subsequent to the events instigated by the Duke of Northumberland, John Dudley and also how she initially treated him despite the fact he attempted to usurp her claim to the throne.

I wanted to form an opinion of the women and see if it really was in her nature to act in the manner I have portrayed in this version of events.

Mary was the first Queen to reign in her own right, her background certainly had the potential to turn any right minded individual into a bit of a screw ball! Mary was born at Greenwich on 18 February 1516, the only surviving child of Henry VIII and Catherine of Aragon. Mary's life was radically altered when Henry divorced Catherine to marry Anne Boleyn. In order to legitimise this course of action Henry claimed that the marriage was incestuous and illegal, as Catherine had been married to his brother, Arthur prior to his death. The pope disagreed with this assertion, resulting in Henry's break with Rome and in very brief summary the establishment of the Church of England.

Henry's allegations of incest effectively bastardised poor Mary. After Anne Boleyn bore Henry another daughter, Elizabeth, Mary was forbidden access to her parents and stripped of her title of princess. Mary never saw her mother again. With Anne Boleyn's fall from grace and subsequent execution there was a chance of reconciliation between father and daughter, but Mary refused to recognise her father as head of the church. However, she eventually agreed to submit to her father and Mary returned to court and was given a household suitable to her position. She was named by Henry as successor to the throne after her younger brother Edward, born in 1537. This was through the Third Act do Succession formally titled the Succession to the Crown Act 35 Hen. VIII c.1, and is also known as Act of Succession 1543.

This Act superseded the First Succession Act (1533) and the Second Succession Act (1536), whose effect was to declare both Mary and Elizabeth bastards, and allow Henry to name his own successor. When Henry's son Edward was born in 1537, he then became the heir to the throne. This new Act returned both of Henry's daughters Mary and Elizabeth to the line of succession, behind Edward, any potential children of his, and any potential children of Henry by his then wife, Catherine Parr.

The Treason Act of 1747 made it high treason to interrupt the line of succession to the throne established by the Act of Succession. However, Edward VI meant to bypass this Act in his "Devise for the Succession", issued as letters patent on 21 June 1553, by naming Lady Jane Grey as his successor in place of Mary. This clearly was heavily influenced by the Duke of Northumberland's input. Prevailing over Lady Jane Grey, Mary ascended the throne per the terms of the Third Succession Act.

This highlights some of the torment that the young Mary had to endure as a girl growing up in a country where her religion so central to her life was simply side-stepped so her father could divorce her mother and remarry someone else of his choosing.

When her brother Edward died Mary had widespread popular support particularly in the East of England where the people were pretty fed up with the reformation and putting down of the Kett rebellion; hence it seemed a logical place to centre a good proportion of the story. Mary would have had good and trusted connections with the area hence siting Jane there.

Once Mary was queen, she was determined to reimpose Catholicism and marry Philip II of Spain. Neither policy was universally popular. Philip was Spanish and therefore distrusted, and as time had passed many in England now had a vested interest in the prosperity of the Protestant church, having received church lands and money after Henry dissolved the monasteries in an attempt to garner popular support where and when he needed it.

In 1554, Mary crushed a rebellion led by Sir Thomas Wyatt. The precise reason for the uprisings has been subject to much debate. Many historians, such as DM Loades consider the rebellion to have been primarily motivated by political considerations, not easily separated from religious ones in the 16th century; notably the desire to prevent the unpopular marriage of Queen Mary I to Philip. He is a pivotal figure in Mary's behaviour. The rebels explained that the reason for the rebellion was "to prevent us from over-running by strangers." Nevertheless, all the rebel leaders were committed Protestants. An informer called William Thomas claimed that the conspirators in fact intended to assassinate the Queen and named John Fitzwilliam as the assassin. However, the Crown at Wyatt's trial acquitted him of any intention to actually harm the Queen.

It is reported in some records that Mary at 37 and many years his senior was infatuated with Philip and making the most of her advantage in quashing the rebellion married Philip, pressed on with the restoration of Catholicism and revived the laws against heresy.

However, it seems that Philip was not really interested in the aging and plain Mary; it was more England and the realm that caught his attention.

Over the next three years, hundreds of Protestants were burned at the stake; whether this was Mary or Philip or his influence that provoked this is less than clear although a heavy inference can be drawn. This created disillusionment with Mary's reign which was deepened by an unsuccessful war against France which led to the loss of Calais, England's last possession in France, in January 1558. Childless, sick and deserted by Philip, Mary died on 17 November 1558. Her hopes for a Catholic England died with her.

We can say with some certainty that she welcomed her extended family as evidenced by having Katherine Grey Jane's sister at court and the accounts of her treatment which seems to be generally positive despite some provocation to the contrary by Katherine. Likewise, her half-sister Elizabeth who seemed to be trouble from the start was generously 'managed' by Mary.

Finally, and it was the part that fascinated me the most about this period of history. Jane was the Queen of England, albeit for only nine days, she was the eldest daughter from a family that had a legitimate claim to the English throne and yet despite there being many pictures of her siblings nowhere is there a verified painting from the time of Lady Jane Grey; that seemed and seems odd to me and required an explanation.

Bibliography and General Reading

Adams, S. (ed.) (1995) *Household Accounts and Disbursement Books of Robert Dudley, Earl of Leicester, 1558–1561, 1584–1586.* Cambridge: Cambridge University Press.

Adams, S. (2002) *Leicester and the Court: Essays in Elizabethan Politics*. Manchester: Manchester University Press.

Alford, S. (2002) *Kingship and Politics in the Reign of Edward VI*. Cambridge: Cambridge University Press.

Ascham, R. (1863) Mayor, John E. B., (ed.) *The Scholemaster.* London: Bell and Daldy.

Bellamy, J. (1979) *The Tudor Law of Treason.* Toronto: Routledge, Kegan & Paul.

Britannia, (1999) Execution. *Britannia.* [Online] Available from:

http://www.britannia.com/history/ladyjane/executon.html [Accessed: 20th February 2015]

Davey, R. (1906) *The Pageant of London.* London: Methuen.

de Lisle, L. (2008) *The Sisters Who Would Be Queen: Mary, Katherine and Lady Jane Grey. A Tudor Tragedy.* New York: Ballantine Books.

Hanson, M. (2015) The Executions of Lady Jane Grey & Lord Guildford Dudley, 1554. *English History.* [Online] Available from: http://englishhistory.net/tudor/executions-of-lady-jane-grey-lord-guildford-dudley/ [Accessed: 8th February 2015]

Hanson, M. (2015) Charles Brandon, Duke of Suffolk and Princess Mary Tudor. *English History.* [Online] Available from: http://englishhistory.net/tudor/relative/charles-brandon-mary-tudor/ [Accessed: 31st January 2015]

Hanson, M. (2015) Lady Jane Grey – Facts, Biography, Information & Portraits. *English History.* [Online] Available from: http://englishhistory.net/tudor/relative/lady-jane-grey/ [Accessed: 1st February 2015]

Hartweg, C. (2012) The Young Earl of Warwick, Part III. *All Things Robert Dudley.* [Online] Available from: https://allthingsrobertdudley.wordpress.com/2012/03/28/

the-young-earl-of-warwick-part-iii/ [Accessed: 31st January 2015]

Ives, E. (2009) *Lady Jane Grey: A Tudor Mystery*. Oxford, UK: Wiley-Blackwell.

Lady Jane Grey Reference Guide, (2015) Letter to Sister. *Lady Jane Grey Reference Guide*. [Online] Available from: http://www.ladyjanegrey.info/?page_id=2372 [Accessed: 20th February 2015]

Loades, D. (1996) *John Dudley Duke of Northumberland 1504–1553*. Oxford: Clarendon Press.

Nicolas, H.N, (1825) *The Literary Remains of Lady Jane Grey: With a Memoir of Her Life*. London: Harding, Triphook & Lepard.

Plowden, A. (2004) *Lady Jane Grey: Nine Days Queen*. Gloucestershire: Sutton Publishing Limited.

The New Encyclopaedia Britannica, (1992) *Ascham, Roger*. 15th ed., Vol. 1, Chicago: Encyclopaedia Britannica Inc.

Taylor, J.D. (ed.) (2004) *Documents of Lady Jane Grey: Nine Days Queen of England, 1553*. United States: Algora Publishing